H̶ ̶o̶p̶... ̶H̶e̶ ̶s̶c̶a̶n̶n̶e̶d̶ the room,
then he looked at Brenda. Her
response was all that mattered.

She shook her head. "It's too big."

His hopes fell. "You don't like it?"

She grinned. "I didn't say that."

All his tension eased. He watched her take off
her coat and hang it on the coatrack. She said
something, but he didn't hear her. He couldn't
believe what she was wearing; he noticed where the
zipper was and knew that in one quick motion, he
could have her out of it.

"Dominic?"

He blinked. "Huh?"

Books by Dara Girard

Kimani Romance

Sparks
The Glass Slipper Project
Body Chemistry

Kimani Arabesque

Table for Two
Gaining Interest
Carefree
Illusive Flame

DARA GIRARD

is an award-winning author of both fiction and nonfiction books. Her love of writing started at a young age. After graduating from college, she decided to write full-time. She enjoys writing romance because of the range it provides, from comedy to suspense. Her novels are known for their sense of humor, interesting plot twists and witty dialogue.

In addition to writing novels, Dara enjoys reading, painting and going for long drives.

Dara loves hearing from her readers. You can contact her at www.daragirard.com, or P.O. Box 10345, Silver Spring, Maryland 20914.

Body
Chemistry
DARA GIRARD

KIMANI
ROMANCE

To those who believe in second chances

KIMANI PRESS™

ISBN-13: 978-0-373-86099-9
ISBN-10:   0-373-86099-4

BODY CHEMISTRY

Copyright © 2009 by Sade Odubiyi

www.kimanipress.com

Printed in U.S.A.

Dear Reader,

Welcome to the third book in THE BLACK
STOCKINGS SOCIETY series.

Do you believe in second chances? Brenda Everton does
not. When she has to ask her ex-husband, Dominic
Ayers, for a big favor, she's only willing to have a business
relationship.

However, Dominic has plans of his own. He knows
that Brenda is the only woman for him and that love
can be sweeter the second time around. The problem is
convincing Brenda to give him another chance.

I hope you enjoy Brenda and Dominic's story.

You can find out more about this series and learn about
my other titles on my Web site, www.daragirard.com.

All the best,

Dara Girard

Chapter 1

Dear Dr. Everton:

We regret to inform you that the National Science Research Board has decided not to fund your project. While we found merit in what you are doing, we were not convinced that you have the staff and facilities necessary for the ongoing development and sustainability of the project beyond the monies you requested.

If you would like to appeal this decision, please go to our Web site…

Brenda Everton calmly put the letter down on her desk. She had no urge to crumple or throw it, but accepted it for what it was: a rejection. She swung around in her chair and stared out her office window. She placed her hands on her arm rest. "Damn," she said in a soft whisper that quickly disappeared in the empty room. She listened to the sound of the clock, which seemed to keep time with the light drizzle of rain outside and the footsteps walking past her closed door. A leaf slammed against her window, its yellow color translucent in the watery autumn sunlight revealing its intricate veins. In the distance, she caught a glimpse of Seattle's majestic Mount Rainier. The wind soon swept the leaf away and Brenda removed her gaze from the window. "Damn," she said again, this time resigned, but no louder than before.

Her simple response gave no indication that the letter meant the end of three years of research, or the possibility that she'd lose her house. But the prospect of homelessness wasn't something to make Brenda panic. She wasn't prone to extreme, uncontrolled emotions. She had the cool, logical mind of a scientist—a biologist to be exact—and she was used to solving problems, or challenges, as she preferred to call them. She would solve this one. She had to.

Although Brenda did not like the idea of losing her home, the prospect of having to end her project was her number one concern. She hadn't gone through years of schooling, taking risks—including mortgaging her house—and putting her social life on hold, to have it end now. *No merit?* What did they mean? It was obvious they just needed an excuse to reject her. She knew that her research project, developing a disease-resistant plankton, would revitalize a failing fishing industry on the entire West Coast. Over the past twenty years, from the Pacific Northwest up to Alaska, there had been a dramatic drop in the number of selected fish species because of pollution and environmental factors that had practically wiped out their key food source. She and her team had worked tirelessly and had finally been able to grow a plankton utilizing a revolutionary technology they had developed. All she needed was two more years of funding, then she would be able to put it on the market and it would pay for itself and more.

Brenda turned back to her desk and stared at the letter, wishing it would reveal the specific answers she needed. What did they mean she lacked the staff and facilities? Why did they think she was applying for the funds in the first place? She had hired the best and although they were small in number, they made up for it with their commitment and research experience. Two researchers had graduated from Ivy League schools.

Failure meant going back to teaching again, and worst of all, explaining to her mother why she had devoted her life to her career instead of getting remarried.

It didn't matter that Brenda had seven brothers, each in different relationships—some beginning and others ending—to keep her mother occupied. As the only girl, her mother worried most about her. Brenda glanced at a wall full of degrees. She knew they weren't enough, and neither was her position as principal investigator and lead scientist on her project, but pleasing her mother had never been easy. If Brenda focused on men, her mother wanted her to focus on her career; if she focused on her career, her mother wanted her to focus on men and right now, her mother wanted a marriage license.

She'd given her that pleasure once before, producing a son-in-law any mother would be proud of but the marriage had been a disaster. Her mother would have to deal with the fact that her only daughter never planned to marry again.

She wanted to make a name for herself. She wanted to make a difference, leave a legacy. This was her chance and Brenda knew this was the project that would succeed, but she needed more money.

Brenda had fought hard to make it in the predominantly male domain of research biologists. Growing up, she'd fought her brothers for recognition in the household and now she fought a larger establishment. Sometimes she wondered if people were against her ideas or her personally.

But right now she had no time for those thoughts. She needed to put personal doubts and prejudices aside. She needed a solution. She needed to talk to someone. Brenda lifted the phone and called her colleague Chuck Lawson. Moments later he entered her office.

Brenda didn't think anything could clash with the color white, but Chuck's checkered yellow and orange tie did a good job. The embroidered name on his jacket looked like *Chock* instead of *Chuck* because the *u* was too close, but it suited him. He was chock full of energy. Chuck was over sixty but moved like a man of forty. "You wanted to see me?" he said, his green eyes wide and his hands clasped together as if anticipating bad news.

He always anticipated bad news. If the sky was sunny he found a cloud, if rain fell he expected a flood. He was a brilliant scientist and—unfortunately—his predictions were usually right.

Brenda lifted the letter and handed it to him. "Read this."

Chuck pulled out his reading glasses and put them on. Brenda could not help noticing how odd he looked in the dainty, deep red, wire glasses. They were obviously a woman's pair, but he'd been so pleased when he'd purchased them neither she or other members on the team had been able to tell him the truth.

Chuck's eyes widened as he scanned the contents

of the letter, and his breathing grew shallow. "We're ruined," he said as though the building threatened to collapse on them. "This is a disaster."

Brenda maintained her soft tone. "This is not a disaster."

His voice rose. "Not a disaster? We need that money. We can't go on without it."

"Control yourself."

He waved the letter, his voice rising to a shriek. "Do you know what this means?"

"Of course I do."

He ignored her. "It means we'll have to stop paying the researchers. No money for the lab. No money for new equipment. No money for upkeep of the equipment we have. No money for—"

"Chuck!"

He blinked.

"I know," she said with an edge of impatience. "Sit down."

He placed the letter on the table as though it were a snake, then rubbed his hands together. "What are we going to do?" He began to pace.

"Do you know the type of people most likely to die in an emergency?"

He shook his head.

"People who panic." She gestured to a chair. "Sit down and breathe."

He grabbed the chair, collapsed into it and stared at her as though she were his life preserver. "You have a plan, right? That's why you called me in here."

At that moment Brenda regretted making that decision. "Not yet," she said with reluctance, but determined to be honest.

He shook his head and groaned. "This is awful." He pulled off his glasses. "It's the end of all of our hard work." He cleaned the lens with his tie.

"Stop saying that. Labeling a problem doesn't help you solve it. Now I need you to relax. This isn't the end for us." She pushed a box of tissues toward him. "Pull yourself together. I need you to be strong."

Chuck grabbed a tissue and wiped his forehead. The room wasn't hot but sweat streamed down his face, making his pink cheeks shiny and dampening the wisps of silvery blond hair that barely covered his bald spot. He would have made a comical figure if she didn't care so much about him, but right now, his worried state bothered her.

Brenda was aware that he'd faced disaster before and it had nearly ruined him. He'd taken another big gamble when he decided to work with her, and she was determined to make sure he ended up okay.

The two had met several years ago at the university when his career was plummeting from bad partnerships and projects, and hers was rapidly growing because of good connections and a famous husband. There were whispers about Chuck's failed experiments, lack of publishing credits and inability to achieve tenure. Their meeting had been an accident. She'd had an appointment to meet Dr. Landson, one of the most esteemed research scientists at the time, but had gone to Chuck's office instead.

They started talking and discovered they had a lot in common. At the time, Brenda was in the process of going through a divorce and desperate to create a new life, apart from her husband's, and needed an intelligent and hardworking partner. Chuck was a perfect choice. She soon discovered that they worked well together. He kept her from being too serious while she kept him focused.

"Everything will work out," she said gently.

He crumpled the tissue in his hand. "I'm not too worried about the project. It's you I'm worried about. You've put everything into this."

Brenda shrugged, trying to be nonchalant about the magnitude of the problem, although she knew it was serious. "I always rise to the top."

"Should we tell the team?"

"No, there's no use worrying them. We have four months' worth of funding left. That should give me enough time." She looked at Chuck's worried face. "I knew this was a gamble when I started."

"But you thought you would win."

"I haven't lost yet," she said working hard to keep any doubt from her expression.

Chuck opened his mouth, then closed it. He grabbed another tissue.

Brenda watched him with growing uneasiness. Chuck was brilliant at solving scientific problems, but he was not a person to call in a crisis. Perhaps it hadn't been a good idea to let him know. She'd made a poor judgment. She hadn't wanted to carry the burden alone, but knew she would have to. Over the years she had discovered that not all men were strong. Her younger brother, Clement, was just like Chuck. He was very kind, worried too much and never stood up for himself. Which explained why at age twenty-eight he was working for a boss who bullied him.

She had to reassure Chuck. Brenda suddenly snapped her fingers, as though something had come to her. "I have an idea," she lied.

Chuck's eyes brightened; he leaned forward, eager. "You do? What is it?"

"I can't tell you yet. It's just in the planning stages, but I'm certain that it will solve all of our problems."

"It will?"

His voice held such hope it made her want to weep. "Yes. I should have thought of it before. I'm sorry I worried you for no reason."

He sighed with relief and threw the tissues away. "That's okay. I knew you would figure out something."

"That's all then."

Chuck stood, then glanced at the letter. "You can throw that thing away. We don't need their money, right?" He looked at her again for reassurance.

Brenda forced a smile. "Right."

He opened the door with his back straight and his head held high, then left.

Brenda buried her head in her hands.

The door opened again. "Brenda?"

She lifted her head and saw Chuck smiling.

"Yes?"

"Don't wait too long to tell me what the idea is. I may be able to help, remember I'm good with grant writing."

"Yes, I know."

He closed the door. Brenda rested her head back and shut her eyes. For the first time in ten years she wished she had a cigarette. She didn't care if she'd have to stand outside in the drizzling rain squeezed into the designated smoking section, in order to fill her lungs with the hot smoke and nicotine high she desperately needed at that moment.

Brenda sat up and glanced at her watch. Wishing was impractical. She couldn't think about smoking now. She needed to think and there was one place where she did that best: Sam's Coffee House.

She began gathering her things and grabbed her jacket. Suddenly, a young man burst into her office. "Thank God you're still here," he said. "I need a big favor and I promise to make it up to you. I don't know when but it will be one day, I promise."

Brenda looked at him with dismay. Kendell Baldwin was a young professor with a habit of buying expensive shoes and cheap jackets. His latest selection matched his brown skin but already sported a tear at the elbow.

"What do you need?" Brenda asked as she continued to gather her things.

"I have ten students I'm supposed to tutor at five o'clock in the library, but I have a professors' meeting and then a seminar. I overbooked again. I know I should have followed your advice and not carried four courses, but I did, so I have to face it."

Brenda closed her briefcase. "I don't—"

He came around her desk, his light brown eyes pleading. Brenda could imagine his female students falling for him. "It's the basics. First year stuff. You won't have to explain much."

Brenda sighed. "Just this once, but then you have to learn how to schedule your time."

"I will, thanks." He kissed her cheek.

"Careful, you'll make your wife jealous."

He laughed. "She'd never be jealous of you."

"Right."

He looked embarrassed. "Wait, I didn't mean it like that."

"I know."

"It's just that you know, you're um…not like other women."

Brenda shook her head in pity. "Stop digging your grave and get out of here."

He rushed out.

She pushed back a strand of her thick, dark hair and adjusted her bun. His words hurt, but they were accurate. She had always worked around men, and their wives and girlfriends never felt threatened by her. For one thing there was her size. She topped nearly six feet and was always considered one of the guys, which didn't bother her. She'd fought hard to be seen as a scientist and not as a woman. Although at times she felt she had succeeded too well.

In her current work environment, she had no one to impress so the emotion quickly dissolved, as did most sad, irrational emotions. She grabbed her things and left.

At the library Brenda regretted saying yes. Only four of the ten students arrived and of the four, only two grasped the concepts she was trying to teach. The biology class was required, so most of the students had little interest in really learning anything besides finding the easiest way to pass the course, and get an A.

Brenda knew she had made a big mistake when she found herself unable to help one student understand the role of recessive genes in the reproductive cycle of the bullfrog and found another student, a tall thin girl with stringy brown hair, busy texting her boy-friend every few minutes.

The experience made her glad she'd stopped teaching. Luckily, one student was attentive. Unfortunately, her interest didn't make up for the rest of the group, but her enthusiasm did make time go by and helped Brenda feel that the entire session wasn't a complete waste of time.

At last it was over. The students left without a goodbye or thank you. Brenda didn't care. The imaginary cigarette was still calling to her. She decided she had to get to the coffeehouse as soon as possible. It was still raining and the one working lamppost outside the library provided less than ample lighting against the dark night as she walked toward the coffee shop, which was just across the street.

"Dr. Everton-Ayers?"

Brenda froze under the overhang outside the library. Nobody had called her by her married name in years. People only knew her as Dr. Everton. She turned and saw a young woman.

"I'm Dr. Everton, yes."

"Oh." The young woman looked down at a book she was holding. "This book says Everton-Ay—"

"Yes," Brenda interrupted. "That was my married name. How may I help you?" she said, trying to keep any irritation from her tone, but she was in no mood to chat at that time of the night. She only cared about getting a cup of coffee and finding a way to get additional funding.

The young woman stood in front of her, blocking her path. Brenda recognized the book immediately: *Biological Illustrations*. The woman awkwardly flipped through the pages and pointed to a pen and ink illustration of a frog. "This is your work, right?"

"Yes, a long time ago." She tried to maintain a calm composure, not wanting to appear too brittle, but could feel her patience begin to wane. *Get to the point*.

The young woman then pulled out a small drawing pad hidden under her coat and shyly showed Brenda a sketch. "I just wondered what you think of this." Brenda looked at the illustration. It was a crudely drawn sketch of a daffodil, which she could barely see under the poor lighting. Unexpectedly, an errant rain drop fell onto the drawing and smudged a line.

It was awful. The proportions were all wrong and unless the girl was trying for impressionism, Brenda knew she should give up the attempt altogether. But at that moment Brenda wasn't in the mood to critique. If she did, she knew her words would be harsh. "You must have an art instructor. Why ask me?" Brenda said politely closing the pad, then pushing it back in the direction of the woman.

"Because I admire you."

"Really?" she said surprised and somewhat pleased.

"Yes."

"Why?"

"Because you were married to Dominic Ayers."

Chapter 2

Brenda wanted to wring the woman's neck as she became more animated. "I just saw him on the Nature channel yesterday and about died. He's gorgeous. You are *so* lucky."

"You mean were. We're divorced."

The woman looked at Brenda as though she were insane. "I can't believe you let him go."

"How did you find out about me?" Brenda asked sharply.

"The Internet of course," the woman said, as though the answer were obvious.

Brenda silently swore. She'd fallen for the ploy.

The young woman wasn't interested in her opinion of her artwork; she just wanted to use them to get close to her, hoping to score with her ex.

"Well, you can be lucky too. He's still single and likes ladies of all ages." Brenda buttoned the top of her coat and began walking, eager to escape the chilly, damp air and rain-soaked sidewalk.

The woman walked beside her. "What is he like? I mean, I know he's gorgeous but he also comes across a little dangerous and wild. Is he?"

Brenda flashed a malicious smile. "He's even more so in person."

"Wow." The woman held her sketchbook close to her chest and closed her eyes.

Brenda rolled her own, then glanced at her watch. "Excuse me." She tucked her leather briefcase under her arm, opened her umbrella, deliberately pointing it in the woman's direction, forcing her to take several steps backward, and hurried across the street fuming. Every time she thought Dominic was out of her life he would barge back in. Why did he have to be so famous?

How could she have known a simple biology graduate would become a respected filmmaker, produce award-winning documentaries, write bestselling books, start two travel companies for the layperson interested in scientific excursions and host an internationally known television series? How could she have known that the man she'd fallen in love with would continue to bury her in the shadow of his acclaim?

She couldn't escape him. She'd always be his ex, something she couldn't ignore or brush aside, no matter how tired she was of people using her to try to get close to him. Unfortunately, it was nothing new. It had been the same during their marriage. If only he'd just remarry and get the scent off of her. But that wasn't her problem right now. Right now she needed a strong drink.

Moments later Brenda sat in Sam's Coffee House, staring down into her second cup of coffee. She liked it black and strong. Nothing fancy. Unfortunately, the coffee hadn't helped her come up with any new ideas. She had six people, including herself, depending on the funding she urgently needed. She'd thought of everything: finding angel investors—she'd already borrowed from close family and friends, venture capitalists, seeking new grantees, or getting a bank loan. Because she wasn't a well-known preeminent biologist, Brenda knew that none of the sources she thought of would work. This award had been her last option. How was she going to come up with 1.5 million dollars in four months, without robbing a bank?

"Dr. Everton," a bright voice said.

Brenda stifled a moan. *Wouldn't anyone leave her alone?* She glanced up and saw Sonya Ling, one of her researchers. For a moment she didn't recognize her out of her lab coat. "Hi."

Sonya sat in the booth unaware that Brenda did not want any company. She was an attractive woman in her mid-twenties and extremely gifted, which is why she was on Brenda's project. Her black hair, which sported streaks of red highlights, framed her petite features.

"I have fabulous news. Bobby, I mean Robert, and I just bought a condo and we've set the date for our wedding. It's going to be in August. You'll get an invitation soon."

Brenda gathered up the energy to look cheerful. "That's fantastic." She was happy for them. Robert also worked on the project.

"I'm telling you now so that you'll make sure your schedule is free so you can come. You *have* to be there."

"Of course I'll come." Brenda took a sip of her coffee, then opened her briefcase hoping to give the impression that she was busy and encourage Sonya to leave.

Sonya stayed. "Oh good. My mother can't wait to meet you. You're the reason Robert and I can get married. After I was removed from Dr. Franklin's project I only had a few options until you hired me and I wouldn't have met Robert either. I love working on this research. I don't know what I would have done if I hadn't found this job. You're a saint."

Right now Brenda felt like the devil. She brushed away the praise. "You were highly qualified. I wasn't doing you any favors."

"Yes, you were. I know that there were two other candidates, who were better qualified, ahead of me. We're all grateful to you. I don't think we tell you that enough but we are and we're thrilled with the progress we're making. It's all so exciting."

"I wouldn't expect less."

Sonya jumped up. "Can I give you a hug? I'm just so happy I need to hug you."

Brenda hesitated, then nodded. "Sure."

Sonya rushed over and hugged her. Brenda remained seated and politely patted her on the back. As Sonya pulled away Brenda could see that she was blinking back tears.

"Please don't tell me you're pregnant too."

"No, I'm not. I'm just really happy." She returned to her seat. "You can bring a date to the wedding if you want."

"I'll probably come alone."

Sonya shrugged and pulled out a little black book from her purse. "Don't you like men?"

"Of course I like men," Brenda said, wondering why she was having this ridiculous conversation with a researcher.

Sonya scribbled something down in her book.

"What are you doing?"

Sonya hid the book on her lap and continued to write. "Just taking down some notes." She looked up at Brenda and grinned. "There are so many things one has to remember when you're getting married." She lowered her gaze and started writing again. "You were married before, right?"

"Yes."

"Ever thought of getting married again?"

"No."

"Why not?"

"Because my marriage was a disaster and I'd prefer not to talk about it," Brenda said when Sonya opened her mouth.

Sonya nodded and put her little book away. "I understand."

Brenda wondered how she could delicately tell Sonya to *Go away*. She opened her mouth to do so when Sonya suddenly gasped. She stared at the *Weekly Science Journal*, which was lying on the seat next to her. She picked it up and began reading. Without any warning, she tapped it, making the paper look as though it were ready to fly. "Can you believe this?"

Brenda silently prayed that it wasn't more bad news. "Believe what?"

"Haven't you read the paper?"

"No, not yet. I was just sitting here hoping for some time by myself and—"

"It says Dr. Franklin won the National Science Research Grant."

Brenda felt her body go cold. "I see."

"He's getting millions for his project. Millions. Are you okay? You look a little ill."

"I'm fine."

"I wouldn't blame you if you were. The thought of that jerk getting all that money makes me ill too. Oh no, there he is."

Brenda glanced over her shoulder. Yes, there he was—tall, proud and handsome, standing at the counter, likely ordering an espresso. He always ordered one with an almond biscotti. He was a creature of habit and one creature Brenda liked to compare to a parasite. He knew whom to latch on to, based on what he needed, and would suck them dry until he found another host. She'd been one of them. His methods had worked and now he was a world-renowned scientist.

Sonya's cell phone buzzed. She checked the number, then jumped up. "Better go. Bye."

Brenda waved and watched her leave. She looked over at Franklin again, desperately wishing she had a cigarette so she could smoke her brains out. What was the use of staying healthy when your life was going into the toilet?

She'd better leave. Brenda gathered her things and headed for the exit. Unfortunately, she reached the door the same time Franklin did. He gallantly held it open.

"Thank you," she said, only because she had to. The rain had stopped but drops still fell from the awning. Three large ones splashed her coat.

He smiled, a smile that used to make her knees weak, but now only made her stomach turn. "You're welcome," he said. "Glad the rain stopped."

Oh damn, he wanted to talk. "Yes." She stared at him. They were the same height, which she loved because he tended to look down on others both figuratively and literally and never had that chance with her.

"I just bought *two* biscotti." That was being dangerously extravagant for him. He liked to keep his body fit and rarely allowed himself to indulge.

She maintained her bold stare. "Great."

"I'm celebrating."

"Uh-huh." She knew he wanted to be congratulated, but she would make him work for it.

"You must not have heard. I won the National Science Research Grant."

"Yes, I heard," she said, sounding bored.

Some of his bravado crumbled as did his smile. "I was chosen out of a total of sixteen hundred applicants. The competition was extremely stiff. Only ten grants were awarded."

"Quite an accomplishment."

His smile returned. That was all the credit his ego needed. "Yes."

Brenda moved past him.

He blocked her. "You know I have to staff this project. Most of the positions are filled, but I could always find a place for you."

She sent him a flat, cold look. "I have a career."

He sniffed. "You have a job supervising that motley crew of rejects for a research project that will likely never be completed."

"They are not—"

"I know you, Brenda. You try to be like the rest of us, but you're not. Everyone knows Dr. 'Loony' Lawson is one day away from a nervous breakdown. And that Ling girl bounces all over the place as though she were about to burst into a cheer."

"She used to be a cheerleader."

"She should have stayed one. She doesn't have what it takes to be a scientist."

Brenda resisted the urge to reply.

He shook his head. "Your researchers are the ones I fired. Not because I'm a bad guy, but because I wanted the best."

Brenda raised her brows and said in a mocking tone, "Even though they were the individuals who helped you get your initial phase one funding?"

"You don't get to the top carrying dead weight. You should have stayed with me. I could have taught you a few things."

"You taught me a lot of things. I'm through learning your lessons and I have no regrets."

"You'll have some soon enough as the years go by and you realize you're in the same place. Think about it." He turned up his coat collar and left.

Brenda watched his confident stride as he approached his expensive, but not flashy, car. She hadn't stood a chance as an undergraduate. She'd fallen for him hard and had thought the world of him until he plagiarized two of her papers. She never let him know that she'd discovered the theft.

At the time of the discovery she realized it was too big a fight for her to win. His career was flourishing and his name was becoming known in the industry. He knew powerful people. She was merely a college junior and knew they would have sided with him. But one day she'd prove him wrong. An unethical parasite couldn't flourish forever and one day he'd be without a host and his career would shrivel up and die.

Brenda went home and popped a TV dinner in the microwave, glad that her craving for a cigarette had diminished. She quickly ate, then decided to take a nice hot shower. The day had been stressful and she still didn't know what she was going to do. Other than

Sam's Coffee House, the shower was another place where she was able to think clearly.

Brenda stripped down, stepped in the shower, then turned on the hot water. A gush of freezing cold water rushed out, hitting her skin like tiny shards of ice. Her body trembled as she waited for it to warm up. It didn't. She quickly shut off the faucet and swore as she grabbed her robe off a side hook. She stomped down into the basement, water dripping everywhere, and checked her water heater. The sight of it confirmed her worse fears—it was broken.

Brenda kicked it with her bare foot, stubbing her big toe. She hopped around swearing, then gingerly set her foot down. Yes, she definitely deserved a cigarette now. She went back upstairs, changed into a pair of black pants and a white T-shirt, threw on her raincoat and drove to the local mini market. She approached the counter. "I want some cigarettes." She held up a hand. "Don't say anything, just give me those." She pointed to the brand she liked.

Mr. Hopkins nodded. He wasn't old, but moved as quickly as a sloth. Brenda gripped her hands into fists, resisting the urge to tell him to hurry up. To divert her attention she looked at the small TV he had mounted on a shelf. An anchorwoman came on the screen, "And Dominic Ayers is donating nearly half a million dollars to the Alaskan Wildlife Foundation. We had a chance to speak with him…"

Brenda turned away so she didn't have to see her ex and began humming to block out his voice.

Mr. Hopkins placed the carton in front of her and rang up the price. "That Dr. Ayers may look intimidating, but he is a good man."

Brenda handed him the money.

"Always helping people and doing good things."

Brenda held out her hand for the change.

Mr. Hopkins continued to count each coin. "I remember when he first came on TV. My daughters didn't care much about science until his show. You know the one, *The Science Is Fun* program that was featured on Saturday mornings. My kids learned a lot. Now they're getting straight A's in science."

He finished putting the last penny in her hand. Brenda thanked him, took the change and left. She drove home knowing exactly what she would do— sit on her patio and smoke. Although her cigarettes called to her while she was driving, she resisted lighting up because she didn't want to smell up her car. The lingering odor of cigarette smoke was one of the reasons why she'd stopped.

Brenda parked her car and rushed inside. She threw her coat on the couch, then went to her patio, ripping the carton open as she stepped out in the still night. She could feel her tension ease as she sniffed the box. Heaven was just a match away. *A match*. She paused. She'd forgotten to buy matches. She checked her kitchen drawers hoping for a miracle—nothing. Then she looked at the stove. That would have to do.

She reached to turn it on when the phone rang. Brenda hesitated, then answered. "Hello?"

"I didn't win the award," Madeline said.

Brenda imagined her friend lounging in her lavishly furnished living room. "That's okay. There will be others."

"Not as many as you'd think."

Brenda frowned. It wasn't like Madeline to sound depressed. "You can try again next year."

"I saw that Fink won the NSR grant."

Brenda laughed remembering their nickname for Franklin. "Yes."

"And Dominic is donating to—"

"Yes, yes," Brenda interrupted. She didn't need yet another reminder of what her ex-husband was up to.

"Remember how we all started out basically the same and look at us now."

Brenda didn't like the direction the conversation was going. "We're all successful."

"Some more than most," Madeline said without interest. "Sometimes I wonder if I've made a mistake with my life."

"Not at all. You are a well respected scientist, you're published and—"

"But is that enough?"

Brenda rested against the counter. "Madeline, is something wrong?"

"No, I was just calling to see how you were doing with the news about Franklin."

Brenda didn't believe her. "I really am sorry about you not getting that award. I didn't get one either."

"So we're both finished," Madeline said gravely.

"No, we'll think of something. Would you like to go out for dinner tomorrow evening?"

"Sure."

Brenda sighed, relieved that Madeline sounded more upbeat. Madeline was more than her best friend, she was her mentor. She was a very attractive woman, with a dark cocoa complexion, impeccably styled shoulder-length hair and a fantastic figure. Food and friends—that's all she needed, Brenda thought. And Brenda could use the company. They could talk about their projects, complain about Franklin, laugh, have a few drinks and then everything would be fine. "Great. I'll call you then."

"Right."

Brenda hung up, then stared at the framed photo taken years ago when Madeline won the International Academy of Natural Science Award. She was only a couple years older than Brenda, but was everything Brenda aspired to be—devoted, dedicated and driven.

Brenda hoped that one day she would accomplish half of what Madeline had done. Madeline had been a prodigy, completing her undergraduate degree in two and half years, and her doctorate in three years. She was a beautiful woman, who hadn't let romance or marriage deter her from her professional aspirations. Brenda smiled, feeling a little better and put the cigarette away. She looked forward to tomorrow; it would make up for today.

"You need a new water heater," her neighbor Lincoln Darnell said as he came up from the basement the next day. She'd called him right after work hoping for better news.

"You can't fix it?"

"Nope." He folded his arms, covering the Seattle Seahawks sweatshirt he liked to wear.

She cringed. "It's going to be expensive, isn't it?"

"Yes, I'm afraid so, but if you want hot water…"

Brenda groaned as she walked with him outside. "Yes, I'll get back to you. Thanks for stopping by."

"No problem. My son got a B on his science project thanks to you."

"He's fun to work with."

Lincoln nodded, waved goodbye and left. Brenda checked her mailbox, then went back inside. She dropped the large bundle on the table, then dialed Madeline's number. She hadn't been able to reach her all day and couldn't reach her now. She hung up the phone, pushing away her concern. Madeline probably had a busy day. She always got back to her; she didn't need to pester her with messages.

Brenda grabbed her mail and sat down at her desk to sort through it. Junk, junk, junk. As each item left her hand it fell into the wastebasket beside her. Then one piece caught her attention. She opened it. It was a handwritten note, on expensive parchment paper, lined with finely woven lace in a gold-lined envelope. It was addressed to Brenda Katherine Everton. Perhaps it was Sonya's wedding invitation, although Sonya had no way of knowing her full name.

She shrugged, then she began to read it, curious.

You have been personally selected to join The Black Stockings Society, an elite, members-only club that will change your life and help you find the man of your dreams. Guaranteed.

Brenda frowned, flipping the invitation over, confused. What was it? She continued reading.

Dumped? Bored? Tired of Being Single?
Ready to live dangerously? Then this is the club
for you. Guaranteed Results! Submit your application today.

Nonsense. She noticed the nominal fee and
specific instructions that she had to submit the application within seven days or she'd lose the opportunity of a lifetime.

Ridiculous. She didn't need this kind of distrac-
tion. Someone probably sent it to her as a joke. She
had enough to think about and didn't need any
pressure to join some stupid society. She tossed the
invitation in the wastebasket along with all the
other junk.

Brenda ended up eating another TV dinner that
evening. Madeline never returned her call. It didn't
bother her, she figured Madeline had forgotten. It
wasn't unlike her friend to forget appointments, especially if she was trying to solve a problem or was busy
with a project. That night Brenda went to bed thinking
of one thing: how to solve her cash flow crisis.

She woke up to a male's voice in her bedroom. It was
low, smooth like melted butter on warm biscuits, beautiful and familiar, with an amusing Canadian accent.

Dominic. Her eyes flew open. Her gaze darted
around the room, then she realized she was alone, but

the voice was still there. She turned to the radio. His voice came toward her as though he were beside her. He was being interviewed on one of the early morning radio shows she loved to listen to.

Brenda slammed the alarm off. It had been a long time since she had woken up to his voice and she didn't need to be reminded of how nice it was to hear. She spent that morning boiling several pots of water, to wash her face and hair, which was in desperate need of a good shampoo. She decided to skip blow drying and put her hair in two large braids instead. It was the weekend and she didn't have to worry about anyone important seeing her, not that she was ever interested in making a fashion statement.

Brenda went outside and retrieved her morning paper, before having her morning coffee and a large banana nut muffin. She only received the daily news-paper on weekends, because she was usually too busy to read it during the week. She sat down at her kitchen table and opened the paper. She nearly choked when she saw the headline: *Renowned scientist Dr. Madeline Cartwright found dead from apparent suicide.*

Rain wasn't unusual in Seattle, so no one let it bother them as they stood around the grave site under a canopy, trying not to get wet. Brenda looked around

and was surprised by the small crowd. Madeline had
known so many people. Had her life diminished to
this? All the faces were a blur. Brenda usually paid
attention to detail but this time she couldn't. The
coffin loomed large in her mind. This couldn't be
real. Madeline was only forty-two. She had so much
more to do. Why had it ended this way?

Brenda wondered if she should have gone over to
Madeline's house the last time they spoke. Was she
reaching out; did Brenda not hear her cry? She had
thought she was her friend. Why hadn't she called
her? Damn, damn, damn.

The brief grave site service came to a close. One
moment the coffin was there, then it was in the
ground. All Brenda remembered was the sound of
dirt hitting the coffin. Madeline was gone.

Brenda walked slowly back to her car. She paused
when she saw a tall, striking dark figure ahead. It was
Dominic. She jumped into her car in case he turned
around and saw her. She needn't have worried; he was
busy consoling Madeline's mother who had cried un-
controllably throughout.

What was he doing here? Shouldn't he be travel-
ing or on some radio show? How could he have remembered Madeline?

Brenda started her car and drove to Madeline's
parents' house to express her condolence. Once there

she was surprised to find a larger group gathered. She overheard several individuals say that they couldn't bear seeing Madeline in a coffin or watching her being lowered into the ground and had decided not to go to the viewing or grave site. Brenda spoke to several of Madeline's business friends, then approached her sister, Dana. "I'm so sorry."

"I can hardly believe that it's real. I didn't sense anything," Dana said, her face reflecting the shock and pain she felt.

Brenda nodded, feeling her wave of guilt resurfacing. She shouldn't have waited for the next day. She should have gone over to see her. Perhaps she could have—

"She wanted you to have this." Dana handed Brenda a small white envelope. She put it in her handbag, stuffing it in-between her carton of cigarettes and wallet. Suddenly, she heard his voice and footsteps. Dominic rarely entered a room quietly and once inside one couldn't help but stare at him. He was as magnificent as a mountain and just as majestic, but his movements were not refined and people easily made the assumption that he came from the backwoods of Canada instead of one its prestigious cities. Brenda knew it was all an act that he used to mislead people to give himself the advantage. When he wanted to, he could move with the noiseless steps of a fox hunting its prey or act as cultured as a prince.

His biography said he'd immigrated to America at fifteen. The truth was that he'd run away to live with an aunt.

Brenda knew she had to disappear before he saw her. She couldn't handle talking to him now. When they had been together they were either fighting or making love. He was the one person who could make her lose her cool. She couldn't afford to, not here. Brenda darted into the next room where the buffet table stood. She lifted a plate, knowing she couldn't eat anything, but needing something to do.

She set the plate down when she heard familiar footsteps come closer. She silently swore. Of course he'd head to the buffet table. The man could eat it clean, although his muscular physique gave no indication of that. There wasn't an inch of fat on him; he was as solid as marble. She disappeared behind a large palm and watched Dominic and Franklin enter. Neither man appeared to notice the other. Franklin's presence didn't surprise her. He would want to be there to console Madeline's family in case there were photographers. She lost sight of Dominic but saw Franklin talking to Madeline's mother and father. At that moment, she wished Madeline was there so the two of them could laugh at him. He was always a comical character to watch, because he thought he was more important than he was, and it showed.

"Are you hiding from me?" a deep voice said behind her.

Chapter 3

Brenda froze, hoping that when she turned it wouldn't be who she thought. She slowly spun around and looked up. Dominic was one of the few men she had to look up to. He topped six-four and was the one man who didn't make her feel anything less than a woman. When she was with him all of her feminine instincts became alert.

From their first meeting she'd responded to his sheer male energy. It wasn't just that he was large, but that he was stronger than her, and his piercing eyes, every bit the scientist's—calculating and assessing— may have intimidated another woman, but always made her skin tingle with anticipation. With his smooth brown skin, shaved head and black goatee, all he needed was a black eye patch and a dark cape to look like an avenging outlaw, ready to relieve you of anything you treasured. He had the charm of a rogue, the eyes of a seducer and a smile that could persuade a woman to say "yes" when she meant the opposite. He had an irresistible magnetism.

Brenda shook away the sensation annoyed with herself. It was these kind of thoughts and unchecked feelings that had gotten her in trouble in the first place. Yes, he was big and strong and brilliant and sexy, but he was just a man and she knew how to handle men.

"Why would I want to do that?" she asked.

He lifted a brow. "Exactly."

"I didn't expect you to be here."

He shoved his hands in his pockets, looking sad. She knew he was. He was never insincere. "God, I wish I wasn't. I can't believe this."

"Me neither."

"I respected her. More than that, I liked her. She was a great woman and a brilliant scientist."

Brenda nodded, grateful for the neutral topic. "Yes, it's such a waste. All of the ideas she had, all the things she could have accomplished."

"All the things she could have experienced."

"What?"

"You're just thinking of her as a scientist. Unfortunately, I think that's the only way she saw herself too. As her mother told me, losing the award devastated her. You can't confuse your profession with who you are."

"Is that a lecture, Dr. Ayers? Don't worry, we didn't consider ourselves asexual robots. The day she died we had planned to go out for dinner and complain about men." Brenda tried to make light of it, but his assessing gaze didn't waver. She sighed; getting him off a topic had always been difficult.

Dominic took her hand. The shock of his large, warm fingers encasing hers nearly paralyzed her. "Honey, I'm sorry."

Her voice shook. "Dominic, if you want me to burst into tears you'll succeed if you look at me like that any longer."

"I just want you to know that I'm here for you."

Brenda tried to tug her hand free. "Yes, I know."

"How are you holding up?"

"I'm fine."

He tightened his grip, not enough to hurt her, but enough to stop her from struggling. "If you ever need to talk about this, call me."

"I'm fine really. Thanks."

Madeline's mother approached them. "It's so good for you both to come together. Madeline had always hoped you two would reconcile."

Brenda widened her eyes, surprised. "But we're not—" Dominic rested his arm on her shoulders.

"I'm amazed at how grief can bring people together. I'd always hoped that she would learn from you, Brenda, and have something else in her life besides work," Madeline's mother said, her eyes red and swollen with grief.

"But her work was revolutionary," Brenda said, not wanting her friend's lifework to be lost in the sadness of her passing.

"And it killed her," her mother replied bitterly then turned and walked away.

"She's wrong," Brenda said annoyed. "Her work didn't kill her, she just…" Brenda shook her head, not able to come up with a good explanation. She glanced at his arm on her shoulders and tried to shrug it way. When she couldn't she said, "What is this for?"

"The thought of us together made her happy. Why tell her the truth now? She's already suffering enough." He placed his hand on the back of her neck and began gently rubbing it.

"What are you doing?" she said through clenched teeth, trying not to enjoy the sensation.

"You know what I'm doing. You're tense."

Brenda moved away. "I'm not that tense." She looked and saw a woman staring at them. The woman's gorgeous features and fine dress looked out of place, like a crystal glass among tin cans. When she saw Brenda she offered a tentative smile.

"Is she with you?"

Dominic glanced back, made a quick motion with his hand, to which the young lady nodded, then walked away. "She's not my girlfriend."

"That wasn't my question."

"No, but I wanted you to know that."

"I won't even ask why because the reason wouldn't matter." She took a step back. "I guess I'll leave now."

Dominic took her elbow and forcefully, yet gently, led her to a nearby couch. He sat and pulled her down beside him. "She works for me and she's seeing Thomas."

"Your cousin?"

"Yes, he's my manager now."

"I'm not surprised. You two were always close."

Dominic glanced around. "He's here somewhere. We're working on developing a new project."

"Which I'm sure will be very successful. I'm surprised you made the time to come here," Brenda said, unable to stop her sarcasm.

"I've learned to make time for things that are important to me."

"Congratulations."

"Is that all?" he said with surprise. "I should get a royal pardon at least."

She frowned. "What does that mean?"

"The Queen is without fault. Everything was my doing. I caused our divorce."

"I never said that."

"You didn't have to."

"Look, I blame myself too, many times, but it's over, so it doesn't matter anymore." She stood. "Goodbye."

He stood too. "Brenda."

She rested a firm hand on his chest and glanced around, embarrassed. "Lower your voice."

"I wasn't shouting."

"You don't think you're shouting, but your voice could be heard in the Everglades."

He lowered it. "I'm sorry." He glanced down at her hand and a slow smile spread on his face. She snatched her hand away.

"Let's not argue," Brenda said, determined to keep her composure. "I know it's something we do well, but let's not do it here."

He leaned forward, a devilish twinkle in his eyes. "There's something else we do well."

Brenda's gaze fell and heat stole into her cheeks as the memory of their lovemaking rushed back to her as though he'd stripped her bare. But she wouldn't let him unnerve her. She boldly stared back. "I know, but we're not going to do it here either." Brenda quickly turned away and marched to the foyer. She swung open the closet door and frantically searched for her coat.

She didn't have much time to look before Dominic spun her around. His eyes, dark like midnight, pierced hers. "Brenda, we need to talk."

The scent of his cologne embraced her, the same cologne that used to cling to their sheets at night and his bath towel in the morning. His hands firmly held her shoulders, hands that used to hold her close when they danced and that caressed her body when they made love.

A sense of the magnitude of her loss hit her as she thought about how Madeline used to visit them for dinner. Those had been fun and happy times. Now they were gone forever. Her eyes filled with tears. "Please don't say anything," she begged, anguish making her voice tremble. "My friend just died."

"I know." He surprised her by pulling her into his arms. She didn't mind. At that moment she wanted to be held. She wanted to be comforted. She wanted to know that she wasn't alone. And she cried because she knew he was strong enough to take her tears. He didn't say anything. There were no soothing words of comfort or reassurances, he was just there—a quiet, solid presence and that was all she needed.

Finally the tears ebbed and she drew away. "Thank you."

He nodded.

Brenda looked up and checked his shoulder. "Not too much water damage." She stared down at his chest, unable to meet his gaze. She touched his tie. "Remember when Madeline and I used to compete to see who could buy you the ugliest tie for your birthday?"

"Yes, she usually won."

"I know. I don't know where she got them."

"Especially that one that moved side to side at the sound of music."

Brenda laughed. "Yes, I remember that one."

"I still have it."

She glanced up surprised.

His voice deepened. "I have all of them."

She opened her mouth to respond, but a voice cut her off.

"Brenda, I've been looking for you," Franklin said. "I wanted a chance to tell you how sad I am."

How sad *he* was as though the rest of them didn't feel anything. Typical Franklin. "Thank you."

Franklin glanced at Dominic. "Hello, Ayers."

Dominic nodded. "Franklin."

Neither man liked the other. Brenda had told Dominic about Franklin, but she didn't know why

Franklin didn't like him. He would have made a good ally.

"I would have put her on my project if I'd known she was so desperate."

Brenda knew he was lying. Madeline did not hide the fact that she thought he was a leech. "She probably would have said no anyway," she said.

"Yes, some people have too much pride."

"Or taste," Dominic said.

Franklin narrowed his eyes, then left.

Brenda turned and retrieved her coat.

Dominic took it from her and held it out. "Promise me if you need *anything* you'll call me."

She slipped into her coat. "Of course."

His hands fell to her shoulders, clamping down like manacles. "No, I want your promise."

"Dominic."

His fingers touched the soft hairs on her neck, his voice softened to a whisper. "Promise."

"I promise. If I need *anything* I will call you."

He released her. "Thank you."

"You're welcome." She opened the door.

"By the way, find another vice."

Brenda turned and saw him holding up her package of cigarettes. She reached for them. "Give those back."

He shook his head and put them in his jacket

pocket. "I won't let you ruin an excellent record. That doesn't sound like *my* Brenda."

"I'm not *your* Brenda. I thought you cared but you were just being sneaky and going through my handbag."

"I do care." He grinned. "Drive safely." He closed the door.

Brenda stared at the door for a few seconds, reluctantly impressed with how he'd tricked her and then walked down the steps.

Natalie Swanson darted out of view when Dominic turned away from the door. She didn't want him to see her. She spoke to the man next to her. "Did you see that?"

"See what?" Thomas Yardwell said, entering something into his electronic organizer.

Natalie sent him an annoyed glance taking in his hard jaw and long lashes. She only slept with him out of absolute boredom and knew that their relationship would soon end, but right now it suited them both. "Dr. Ayers and that woman."

That information caught his attention. "Dominic's with a woman?"

"Not now. She's gone." But in the two years she'd been working for Dr. Ayers she'd never seen him look at a woman like that, let alone given Natalie the "I'm okay" signal. Usually it was SOS and she would come to his rescue, efficiently whisking him away from the ongoing rush of unwanted female attention.

"I'm sure it's no big deal," Thomas said.

He was blind to anything but work and as Dominic's right-hand man, he had plenty to do. He was responsible for Dominic's busy schedule, which was constantly full. Dominic didn't seem to mind, but Natalie worried about him. Not that anyone listened to her; she was just an assistant and a girlfriend. Thomas wasn't interested in her opinions. He liked three things about her: her looks, her money and her father's name.

The Swanson name opened doors for him and Thomas treated her well because of it, as though she were an investment. She didn't care, because she liked being treated well. Although she didn't need the assistant job Thomas had gotten for her, she liked being useful and working for Dr. Ayers was never boring.

For a while she thought Dominic wasn't interested in women in that way. He flirted with them, but never went beyond that. Seeing him today erased that thought.

When she saw him talking to that tall, intimidating figure, who she later discovered was Brenda Everton, she thought it was just business, but that assumption changed when she noticed the way Brenda looked at him. At first she guessed he might need rescuing until she saw how he looked back at Brenda and the look made Natalie's eyes widen with shock. "I wonder if they're still in love."

"Who?" Thomas asked, all interest gone.

Natalie walked away. "Never mind."

Brenda woke up to the phone ringing. She glanced at the clock, but her eyes were swollen from crying and she could barely make out the time. She picked up her wrist watch and squinted. It was one o' clock. From the sun peering through the blinds it was obviously one in the afternoon. The fact that she'd overslept didn't matter because she'd taken the day off. Madeline's letter still lay on the ground where she'd left it last night. The phone continued to shrill. She grabbed it and grumbled, "Hello?"

Her brother's soothing voice came on the line. "It's Clement. I wanted to make sure you're okay."

"I'm okay," she said trying not to sound too surly. She knew he cared but she was sick of being asked the question. He lived alone in Portland, Oregon, but occasionally came to visit. He was one of the few brothers who bothered to find out how she was doing, the rest were too busy.

"I'm really sorry about Dr. Cartwright. Her whole life was her career and when it didn't work out she gave up."

"She was my idol."

"That's what worries me."

Brenda sat up. "Why?"

"You don't think you're similar?"

Brenda rubbed her eyes. "I'm not going to kill myself if that's what you're thinking."

"Picked up any cigarettes?"

This was why he was her favorite brother and why he also annoyed her. "Do you have spies?"

"I know you and I know how you used to deal with stress."

"I haven't smoked yet, I just thought about it. I have a lot on my mind."

"Like what?"

"It doesn't matter." Brenda was in no mood to tell Clement about the money she needed for her project and that she was just as desperate as Madeline had been. It would only confirm his comparison of them.

"It's work-related, isn't it?" he asked, sounding smug.

"Actually it's about the three men I'm currently dating. They're all scheduled to come over today and I don't know what to do."

"Uh-huh."

His tone made her defensive. "I like my job and I care about the people who work for me."

"Yes, but you've lived your life these past few years thinking of everyone but yourself. It's not good for your health. When was the last time you were on a date or took a vacation?"

"I don't remember."

"Brenda, I think—"

"I will go on a vacation soon." She wanted to ask about *his* love life—she knew he didn't have one—or his bully boss, so he would realize his life was as stagnant as hers, but she didn't want to argue. "I'd better go, there's someone at the door. Talk to you later." Brenda hung up the phone. She contemplated going back to bed, but knew she wouldn't be able to get back to sleep. She stood and grabbed her robe then lifted Madeline's letter off the ground and reread it.

Dear Brenda,

Please don't judge me too harshly. After I found out that I lost the funding I knew my life wouldn't mean much anymore. My career was all that I had. I gave it everything and it swallowed my life. I had nothing left and nothing else to live for. It's easier this way. I've let people down and disappointed them and I can't face that. I will miss you. Take care.

Your eternal friend,
Madeline.

Brenda carefully folded the note and put it in her pocket. She went into the kitchen, made a cup of coffee, then stepped out on her patio. She looked out at Lake Washington, which she could see from the back of her house, and watched several boats adrift in the distance. She saw a couple walking along the jogging path, their joy almost palpable.

She thought of Sonya getting married and the joy of starting a new stage in her life. The thought made her feel old. How pathetic, she hadn't completed her third decade yet, although that was close, and she already felt ancient. Work was her life. She couldn't remember the last time she had taken time out to sit and do nothing. She didn't want to end up like Madeline or go back to smoking and being more manic than before.

She needed to change. For a moment she thought about how nice it would be to have a man in her life again. Someone she could talk to, do things with and have incredible lovemaking. That would be nice. She missed it.

But what could she do to change?

Dumped? Bored? Then this is the club for you!

The words popped into her mind. Where had she heard them before? Brenda searched her mind, then remembered. Oh yes, that invitation. She'd thrown it in the wastebasket. It expired in seven days. She counted off the days on her fingers. She had one day left. Her heart raced. Could she? Should she?

Brenda dashed inside, went to her desk and checked the wastebasket—empty. Suddenly panic gripped her. Of course it was empty. Today was trash day.

Chapter 4

Brenda raced outside and heard the roaring engine of the garbage truck as it crawled its way up the street. She lifted the cover from the trash can and started sifting through its contents. She gingerly pushed aside some rotting food escaping a plastic bag and swatted away a couple of flies. She held her breath and continued searching for the small white garbage bag. The truck drew closer, grinding and shifting gears as it stopped and started again.

At last she found the bag and yanked it out, just as the truck pulled up. The driver gave her a wink and a lascivious look, appreciating how her black robe hugged her figure and the vulnerability of her bare feet. She didn't take time to notice.

Back inside she opened the bag, glad that everything was still intact. When she finally found the crumpled invitation, she smoothed it out against her leg, then sat at her desk and grabbed a pen. She read the instructions again, then began to fill it out. Some of the questions would have made her pause before, but she didn't have the time to think them over, and instead wrote down the first thing that came to her.

Which do you prefer?

Postcards or love notes? Postcards.

Flowers or candy? Neither. I prefer something I need.

What would your ideal man be like? Ideal man? Franklin had once been her ideal, but had been her first mistake. Clever, driven and handsome, but he had proven to be all wrong. Dominic had also been her ideal. Brilliant, funny, successful, but he had also turned out to be a mistake.

She wasn't sure she had an ideal anymore; unfortunately she had to write something. She didn't want their complete opposites—a stupid, cruel man. Perhaps the third time would be the charm. Dominic had been a huge improvement over Franklin. Perhaps her new man would be an improvement over Dominic. She wrote: *Intelligent*. Then scratched it out and wrote

Brilliant, attractive, successful, knows how to have fun, and a great lover. She bit her lip, then hastily scribbled down *and loves me more than his career.*

Work had been Dominic's mistress. She didn't want another relationship like that.

Brenda carefully read the "sworn oath" at the bottom of the page: *As a member of The Black Stockings Society, I swear I will not reveal club secrets, I will accept nothing but the best and I will no longer settle for less.*

She checked over her answers, then drove to the post office and mailed it. The moment she released the envelope in the slot she began to doubt her decision. I'm crazy, she thought. I just signed up for a society I've never heard of. She had enclosed a check, although the amount was nominal, but she had no way to trace it. She shrugged. If she got no reply it would fit with the kind of luck she'd been having lately.

"Sad business about Dr. Cartwright," Chuck said when Brenda returned to work.

"Yes," Brenda said, walking to her desk.

He wrung his hands and stared at her. Because he made no motion to leave her office Brenda guessed he had something else to say. "What is it, Chuck?"

"I don't want to bother you, especially after all you've been through."

"But…"

"But I was wondering how your idea is coming. It's not to put pressure on you—I'm just curious. Could I get a hint?"

"No. I'll tell you when everything is settled." Brenda rested her paperwork on her desk and sat down.

"Are you sure there's nothing I can do?"

"Yes."

"I wouldn't mind—"

A knock on the door cut him off.

"Come in," Brenda said, grateful for the interruption.

Sonya bounced in. She handed something to Chuck. "There you go, Dr. Lawson." Then she bounced over to Brenda's desk and placed an envelope on it. "And that's for you, Dr. Everton."

"A wedding invitation," Chuck said reading his.

"Yes. I know I'm supposed to mail them, but I thought this was better. And I get to save two stamps."

"Better yet, you could have saved the environment and just sent an e-card," Chuck said.

Sonya's face fell.

Brenda sent him a cutting glance and he went red. "But you can't put an e-card in a scrapbook," she said.

Sonya's smile returned.

"Right," Chuck grumbled.

Sonya came around the desk and peered over Brenda's arm. "Do you like it? I designed it myself."

Brenda edged her chair away. "It's very nice."

Sonya returned to the other side of the desk. "I already have both of you down as definitely coming. This is just a formality. Please let me know by the deadline if you're planning on bringing a date..." Her words died away as she looked at Brenda, as if the idea were absurd.

"I'll let you know," Brenda said filling the awkward silence.

"Thanks." She bounced out.

Brenda watched her go, reluctantly remembering Franklin's snide remark about Sonya's cheerleading past.

"Can't remember the last wedding I went to," Chuck said.

Brenda looked at the rainbow-colored invitation. "I have a feeling you'll remember this one."

"Have you ordered the water heater?" Lincoln called out to Brenda as she checked her mail. "They're having a sale at the hardware store."

"I'll get to it."

"Better hurry, the sale ends soon."

"Thanks," she said absently, her attention focused on a package left on her doorstep. It looked ordinary, but she knew it was not. She picked it up, anxious to see what was inside. She sat at the kitchen table and opened it. Inside were several items: four pairs of stockings, a membership card and strict instructions. She read the card: *Brenda Katherine Everton, Member, The Black Stockings Society.* It looked very impressive, helping to push aside some of her lingering doubt. Then she pulled out a pair of stockings and burst into laughter. She pulled out another pair and laughed even harder. She could hardly sit up straight when she saw the third pair.

This *had* to be a practical joke. These couldn't be for her. Didn't they know who she was? She was certain she'd been very specific in her application. This was all wrong. She wiped away the tears that had been streaming down her face from laughter and read the letter inside:

Welcome to The Black Stockings Society. Your first assignment is to take your membership card to Big and Beautiful.

B and B? Brenda avoided shopping at that store. She hated any place set aside for women too wide or too tall for regular fashions. She always felt awkward because she didn't know how to shop for clothes. Brenda paused, reconsidering her aversion to Big and Beautiful. Shopping there would be better than going to a regular clothing store. She remembered an incident when she was in her early twenties where a clerk nearly fainted when she'd asked for a pair of black fitted trousers. The woman had looked at her as though she were a giant. B and B may not be too bad after all.

But then again, what was wrong with her clothes? She had her system down. During graduate school, she had been introduced to a tailor who made her custom clothing. Brenda wore primarily black or white, with only a few gray or dark blue items, so that she never had to worry about matching.

Besides, she had spent over ten years working in laboratories wearing a white lab coat. Clothing was not a priority for her. Aside from limiting herself to basic colors, Brenda had no idea of how to select styles that fit her shape. She left that job up to her tailor, and he had done a great job.

Brenda read the instructions again, then shrugged. She could do this. What was there to lose? Flash her membership card and get some new clothes, which she would make sure matched her color scheme. How hard could that be?

Several days later Brenda stood in the large warehouse-like atmosphere of Big and Beautiful, where mannequins loomed large and clothing hung at eye level. She glanced around and found the Customer Service counter. A striking, tall woman stood there looking bored. When she saw Brenda approaching she perked up and smiled. "How can I help you?"

"I believe I'm suppose to show you this." She held out the card.

The woman took the card, then grabbed a pair of scissors.

"Wait. What are you doing?"

"Making sure this is the real thing. Some women have tried to make copies. Don't worry, if it's real, it will pass the test."

She conducted her test, nodded then replaced the scissors. She handed it back to Brenda. "I notice you don't wear heels."

"They're not comfortable. Besides—"

"You don't like towering over people I bet. You'll get over that." She snapped her fingers and an older woman rushed up to them. "Take Dr. Everton to the lounge," she said enunciating the word.

"Yes, yes. Follow me. I'm Mrs. Gilbert."

"I'm Brenda."

"Glad to meet you."

Mrs. Gilbert led Brenda to an elevator. Once the doors closed she punched several numbers into the keypad and the elevator descended. When it eventually opened, Mrs. Gilbert led her down a small corridor, then stopped in front of a dark red door. She knocked, said "Goodbye," then hurried away.

Seconds later the door opened and a woman around Brenda's age, with olive-toned skin, and sharp, pointy features, popped her head out. "What are you doing down here?"

"Someone, I mean Mrs. Gilbert brought me down here."

The lady remained partially hidden behind the door. "Do you have identification?"

"I have my driver's license."

"That's not what I mean. Something that you showed to them up there." She pointed up. "That had someone lead you down here." She pointed down.

"Oh, you mean this?" Brenda handed the woman her card.

"Yes." She inspected it, then said, "That silly woman, she's supposed to take you to the lounge. She's going to get fired."

"She seems sincere," Brenda said, not wanting to be responsible for Mrs. Gilbert losing her job.

"That's not good enough." The woman turned and said something to someone inside, then looked at Brenda. "I'm Marci Jacobs. Follow me."

Brenda tried to hide her surprise when the woman emerged. Her protruding belly made it out of the door before the rest of her. She caught Brenda's look and proudly patted her stomach. "Enormous, isn't it? His father's really tall, so it's expected. I'm not even due for another three months. I wonder what I'll look like then?"

Brenda wasn't sure whether to offer her pity or congratulations. "You must be happy."

"We're thrilled. I never thought this would happen to me."

Brenda made a noncommittal sound, then changed the subject. "Are you part of this Society thing?"

"It's not a *thing* and no, I'm not a member, but I am an associate and I take my responsibilities seriously."

"How can you be an associate and not a member?"

"Easy. The process of selection is the same. I just don't get certain privileges."

"And that doesn't bother you?"

"No. This Society has helped a lot of women and I'm proud to be a part of it."

"But does it really need all this secrecy? I mean it seems a bit overdone for just getting a bunch of clothes and meeting a guy."

Marci stopped walking and turned, looking directly into Brenda's eyes. In one moment she switched from looking like Mother Earth to a Warrior Woman. "This Society is very serious and if you just want to see it as a bunch of clothes and makeup, and meeting some guy, then I suggest I take you back upstairs right now."

Brenda opened her mouth to protest, but Marci

continued. "This club is for women who want to change their lives, who have the courage to do what they have to, to find the love they want. There's power in being a member of The Black Stockings Society. That's why you can't tell anyone." She turned and continued walking.

"When invitations are sent out how does the Society know that the women selected will keep it a secret?"

"We have spies." She smiled. "We know more about you than you think Dr. Everton."

"Can someone find out why they were chosen or who nominated them?"

"No, that's immaterial. You were selected, just accept that and follow the instructions. Women, such as yourself, are selected based on very strict criteria."

Finally Marci stopped in front of a green door and keyed in a number. Brenda briefly wondered if she had dropped into Alice's Wonderland with all the different colored doors. The door opened. Marci flipped on the lights, revealing a large number of racks with an array of clothing items and accessories.

Brenda looked at them with mild panic. "Where's the black?"

"There's no black and no white here. You will be wearing color from now on." Marci could see and feel Brenda's anxiety. "Don't worry. The items that have been selected for you will complement your existing wardrobe. We consulted with Mr. Anthony, your tailor, to help with our selection. Matching the items won't be difficult; your new pieces will all be interchangeable. He also informed us that you're used to having your clothes delivered so we will also continue that service for you."

"I see," Brenda said, unconvinced.

"No, you don't, but you will." Marci walked around Brenda, looking her up and down. "You have beautiful hair. Do you ever wear it down?"

"Rarely. Except in a ponytail. It's so dry and flyaway."

"I'll show you how to control it by wearing broad, classy headbands. You need to let your hair out, especially on weekends, for a different look."

Brenda touched a purple blouse. "I don't think this color looks good on me."

"Don't worry, it will work."

"I think I need shorter sleeves."

"No, you don't. I have selected every item you see here and trust me, they work for your build and body shape."

After hours of trying on several of Marci's selections Brenda still hadn't been reassured, and did not trust Marci's judgment with some of the items. However, if wearing an assortment of colors would help her find her ideal man, she was willing to do whatever it took.

Brenda took copious notes. She did not want to forget anything. She detailed each item Marci selected, including specific instructions for which accessories she should wear with each outfit.

"This fitted long-sleeved turquoise blouse will be able to go with many items in your wardrobe," Marci said, with a heavy sigh as she watched Brenda's hand race across her notepad.

"Which ones exactly?" Brenda asked.

"Any. You can't go wrong. Remember your basic colors are black and white."

"I know that," she said with impatience. "But that particular shade of turquoise appears to be too subdued to wear with something black, and definitely too loud to wear with anything white. And—"

"That's enough!"

Brenda held out her hands, sending a worried glance to Marci's stomach. "Don't excite yourself."

"I'm not going to go into labor, although it's possible, because you're driving me crazy. I have been doing this for years and never in my life have I met someone like you."

"I don't understand."

"The notes, the questions. They're just clothes. So what if one day you don't match?"

"I'm a professional. How I conduct myself is very important. I don't want to come across as some, some…" Brenda tried hard but couldn't find the word.

Marci didn't give her time to find it. "Top business people have been known to wear two types of shoes to work, or have gone to the office with their trouser leg stuck in their sock. It's not the end of the world. Lighten up. You're too hard on yourself."

"But—"

"New rule. No more questions. You have to trust me."

Marci walked to one of the clothing racks near by and pulled out an outfit. "This is what you will wear on your first date."

"My what?" Brenda asked, barely able to register what Marci had said and what she was holding up.

"Date. You're going on one shortly. For dinner. You'll wear your first pair of stockings, the seamed black stockings with a sequined rose embossed on the ankle and this." Brenda looked at the red two-piece tailored suit.

"You have to be kidding. I'd never—"

Marci narrowed her gaze. "Trust me."

Brenda bit her lip. She never wore the color red. Her mother constantly reminded her that red was too loud a color for a woman her age. And whenever she wore a suit, it was always a pantsuit. With her height, her mother had repeatedly pointed out when she was growing up that her long skinny legs looked like corn stalks.

"It's you," Marci said, not giving her a moment to respond. "We'll ship everything to you. Good luck." Marci opened her arms for a hug.

Brenda hesitated, wondering how she was supposed to maneuver herself around Marci's stomach, and she didn't feel comfortable giving her a hug straight on.

Marci tilted her head to the side and let her arms fall. "I make you uncomfortable, don't I?"

Brenda felt her face grow hot. "No, it's not—"

"This Society isn't about wives and mothers if that's what's worrying you. We're not giving you clothes and accessories just so you can get a man. The time we've spent selecting these items was done with a great deal of thought. For a real change to happen in your life you need to get in touch with you and what you want. You joined the Society because you want a man in your life, right?"

Brenda started to respond, offended by Marci's description of her as some desperate single, but Marci continued. "There's nothing wrong with expressing that desire. It doesn't make you weak." Marci walked Brenda to the door. "It took me a while to learn that lesson. You've spent your life fighting so much for everything that you've denied yourself many of life's pleasures. It's time you stopped fighting and started making love. It's a lot more fun." She winked.

Brenda laughed, feeling more relaxed than before. She hugged Marci, glad she understood. "Thanks."

"Don't leave yet. We're not done with you." She handed Brenda a card, and told her she had an appointment at the hair salon behind another door.

With the help of a petite, energetic stylist and beauty consultant, Brenda learned about taking care of her skin, how to apply makeup for a natural look and had her hair done. She emerged wearing her hair in a smooth style that went past her shoulders.

"Wow, is that me?" Her hair felt soft to the touch and for the first time, in a long time, looked healthy and tamed!

"Don't forget, moisture is very important for your hair, and your hair is delicate. Just because it's thick doesn't mean you shouldn't be gentle with it."

At the end of the hair and makeup sessions, Brenda received a full body massage, manicure and pedicure.

"How much do I owe?" she asked the stylist, as she prepared to exit.

"It's all part of the membership. We'll send you six months' supply of beauty products. They'll come with your clothes when they are delivered. Enjoy the rest of the day."

Brenda wanted to share her new look with Marci, but she'd left for lunch. Disappointed, Brenda followed Mrs. Gilbert back upstairs and left.

The clothes and other items arrived at her house that evening and Brenda immediately put them away. Although clothes didn't interest her, she kept her closet organized. She took time to put the colorful items such as scarves, belts, sweaters and shoes in close proximity to the appropriate black and white items.

Once finished, Brenda made some soup, then flopped down on her couch. She grabbed the remote and turned on the TV. She began flipping channels, and there he was: Dominic. It was a rerun of one of his early documentaries. *If you need anything just call me.* She thought of the Society and a chance at a new beginning.

Yes, she needed something and she definitely knew whom to call.

Chapter 5

She shouldn't have tried to hide from him, Dominic thought. He sat at his desk with his feet on the table absently listening to Natalie give him his messages and remembering the funeral. No, Brenda shouldn't have tried to hide from him. He would have left her alone otherwise, but that one action had put his predatory instincts in overdrive. If she wanted to hide, he was going to seek. And it surprised him how glad he was to find her.

He toyed with the yo-yo in his hand, amazed at his response to her. She was a little older and cooler, but she still made his blood run hot. Nothing had changed those deep brown eyes, smooth skin and body, which still suited him perfectly. He hadn't held her only to comfort her; he liked having her in his arms again.

He swore. He should have gotten over her by now. It had been three years. He'd given up hope that she'd ever come back to him and he definitely wouldn't beg.

"Dr. Ayers?" Natalie said.

"Yes?"

"You haven't answered my last question."

He watched the yo-yo go up and down. "What is it?"

"The Board wants to know if you'll speak at the unveiling of the pavilion at Children's Hospital next Saturday."

"Sure." The yo-yo went up.

"You have a two o'clock appointment with Dr. Haag the marine biologist from Sweden, who is in town for a conference."

"Okay." The yo-yo went down.

"Brenda Everton asked that you return her call."

"Fine."

"Your accountant needs to schedule a time when you and he can meet, or at least talk over the phone."

"Okay." He paused, then his feet crashed to the floor and he sat up. "What did you say?"

"That your accountant needs…"

He waved his hands impatiently, pulling the yo-yo

from his finger and letting it clatter on his desk. "No, before that."

She glanced at her notes. "That Brenda Everton asked that you return her call."

"Yes." He wiggled impatient fingers. "Please give me that message." He took it from her and stared at the note. "Yes, I heard right," he said with wonder. "You said Brenda Everton."

"Is there a problem?"

"No, at least I don't know. What did she sound like?"

"I'm not sure. She was very direct."

"Not depressed?"

"No, very controlled."

He nodded relieved. "Yep, that's my Brenda."

Natalie looked at him both curious and intrigued. "I could handle this for you if she's a bother."

He shook his head then looked up at Natalie and grinned at her concerned expression. "I've been wanting this woman to bother me for three years."

"Would you like me to read your other messages?"

"Um…no. Just leave them." She placed them on the table, then left. Dominic slowly sank back in his seat. *What did Brenda want? What was she up to?* He picked up his yo-yo. He had to approach her with the right strategy. *What should he say?* Heard that you called? What's wrong? What do you want? He'd follow her cues, if she was cool, he'd be cooler.

Dominic lifted the phone receiver and began to dial.

Natalie rushed into the room. "Dr. Ayers?"

"I'm on the phone," he snapped.

"I know, but it's an emergency. I have Mr. Woods from Science In The News on the line."

"Can't you take a message?"

"He said it's urgent. One of the hosts for this evening's live TV broadcast had a terrible accident, and he needs a replacement immediately."

Damn, he'd have to fly out immediately if he was going to do it. Richard Woods was a very good friend of his and wouldn't have called him if he didn't have to.

Dominic swore and slammed down the phone.

"They said the host will be all right and you'll be compensated handsomely," Natalie said quickly, mis-interpreting his anger.

"Fine." He stood and grabbed his things. Brenda would have to wait.

Three days. She'd been waiting for a response from Dominic for three days. Brenda sat in her living room, fuming. Nothing. Not a phone call, not an e-mail. Not even sky writing. No reply. *Call me if you need anything.* She'd been foolish to believe him. Each day was a reminder of why Dominic was her ex-husband. He was always busy. Why would this time be any different? She was probably at the bottom of his list of priorities. She'd been so preoccupied, she hadn't tried on any of her new outfits and went to work dressed as usual. Once the ordeal was over regarding where to find funding, she would start wearing them, but presently she was too angry.

The phone rang.

She stared at it. *Don't get your hopes up—it's not him,* she reminded herself.

It rang again.

She answered. "Hello?"

"Hello, this is Natalie Swanson. I'm calling on behalf of Dr. Ayers. He'd like to know if you're free for dinner Friday."

"Yes," Brenda replied. Finally he had found time to put her on his schedule. She tempered her excitement. She didn't care; all she wanted was to meet with him, ask him for a loan and leave. Why did he want to meet over dinner? "Where does he want to meet me?"

"He said he'll send a car for you around 7:30 p.m."

"Thank you, but just send me directions. I'll drive myself."

"It will be at his house," she said tentatively.

"That's fine."

"Are you sure you don't want a car?"

"I'm sure. Thank you."

"You're welcome." Natalie put down the phone, then glanced up when Dominic entered the reception area. He passed her desk and walked directly into his office. He looked exhausted. She knew he had completed the TV show, then visited the original host in the hospital. She also knew he'd been so busy he hadn't attended to details like returning Brenda's call. "I just spoke to Brenda," she said as she took a chair in his office.

He grabbed his yo-yo. "Yes?"

She licked her lower lip. "About the dinner you wanted her to have with you."

"Dinner?"

"Yes, remember you asked me to set one up for you for Friday at 7:30?"

He set the yo-yo down. "I did?"

"Yes," she said firmly, determined that he would not uncover her ploy.

He folded his arms, uncertain. "Did she agree?"

"Yes, she'll meet you at your place."

His brows shot up. "Brenda's willing to come to my house?"

"Yes."

He let his arms fall. "Good." He smiled and looked a little brighter. "Thanks."

Natalie grinned, pleased with herself. "You're welcome."

* * *

That Friday evening, Brenda dressed with care as she put on the red suit. Then she tried on the pair of black stockings with the red rose. They felt luxurious, clinging to her skin and outlined her legs, making them look curvaceous for the first time in her life.

She looked in her full-length mirror and hardly recognized herself. She had pulled her hair back into a French braid. The hair products she had been given made her hair easy to style. A pair of pearl-drop earrings decorated her ears and a thin silver necklace with a large pearl pendant graced her neck. But it was the red suit and black stockings that stunned her most.

A naughty smile touched her face. Dominic was in for a surprise.

"Alliance Incorporated is waiting for a response," Thomas said, straightening one of the awards that lined Dominic's office.

Dominic threw his yo-yo in the air. "I know."

"You can't keep them hanging on."

Natalie knocked on the door, then peeked inside. "Dr. Ayers?"

Thomas rushed over to her and said in a low voice. "I thought I told you to go home over an hour ago. We're busy here."

"I know, but I have to speak to Dr. Ayers."

"Talk to him on Monday."

"But the time," she said sounding a little desperate.

"I know what time it is, but I have to convince him of this deal." He gently but firmly spun her around. "Go home."

"But Thomas—"

He closed the door in her face and turned back to Dominic. He sat in front of him. "Now about Alliance—"

Dominic shook his head as he lounged behind his desk. "Don't worry. I'll give you a decision soon."

The phone rang. Thomas lifted it before Dominic could.

"Not now," Thomas said knowing who the caller was.

"Let me talk to him," Natalie pleaded.

Thomas hung up the phone and turned the ringer off.

Dominic frowned. "Who was that?"

"Nobody." He leaned on the desk and smiled at Dominic, determined to persuade him. If Natalie would just give him time, he knew he could. "I think we should go over the reasons why this is a good career option."

Dominic's cell phone rang. Thomas gripped his hands into fists wanting to smash it under his heel.

Dominic looked at the number and frowned. "It's Natalie. Maybe she—"

"Don't answer it. She's just trying to annoy me because I owe her something."

"She's calling my phone to get to you?" Dominic asked.

"Yes, I turned mine off."

"But—"

"Let's just end this talk, then I'll make it up to her."

Dominic shrugged, then set the phone down. "There's not much to say." He knew that Thomas thought the deal with Alliance Inc. would be great, but Dominic had his reservations. Madeline's death and seeing Brenda again made him want to rethink his helter-skelter lifestyle.

"Perhaps you need more time to think this over."

"Yes."

Thomas sighed, then looked at the clock. "I'd better go. Natalie and I are going out of town tomorrow."

Dominic frowned. "But tomorrow is Friday."

"Today's Friday. Check your calendar."

Dominic's stomach fell as he glanced at his watch in horror: Eight o'clock. "It can't be Friday."

"Why not?"

He jumped to his feet and quickly gathered his things. "Because I was supposed to meet someone at seven-thirty on Friday."

Thomas grinned. "Then you'd better hope that someone is very forgiving."

Moments later Dominic sped down the road while talking to Sheila, his housekeeper, through his earpiece. "Is she still there?"

"Yes."

"Is everything ready?"

"I'm always ready," Sheila huffed.

"Right, of course. You're the best," he said, not wanting to anger two women in one day. "Tell Brenda I'll be right there."

"I've been telling her that. Could you be more specific?"

"Less than twenty minutes."

"Hmm…" Sheila said, unimpressed.

He slowed down for a stop sign. "Does she look upset?"

"No, she looks very calm. You wouldn't think you were late at all."

Dominic swore, then put his foot on the gas. "That means she wants to cut off my—never mind. I'll be there soon."

"He'll be here soon," Sheila said to Brenda in an apologetic tone. Sheila didn't look like a house-keeper, she had the body of a barmaid, the face of a raisin and the chirpy voice of a sparrow.

"Thank you," Brenda said.

"Do you need anything?"

"No, I'm fine."

Sheila nodded, then went into the kitchen.

Brenda glanced around the living room again. Yes, it was all too familiar: the emergencies, the late meetings, the forgotten appointments. If she didn't need his money so much she would have left long ago and kept him out of her life another three years. But she did need him and would do whatever was necessary.

Not that she had much choice of leaving, she thought, glancing down at the Great Dane called Sergeant that had fallen asleep on her feet. When she had arrived, he had followed her and immediately fell on her feet as though he meant to keep her there until his owner returned. She once tried to nudge him to move, but he produced a surprisingly fierce low growl, so she decided it was best to wait for Dominic's return. But she hadn't expected her wait to have been that long.

The dog had surprised her. They never had time for pets, but from the size of his house a lot had changed. It was nothing like the apartment he used to live in or the colonial home they had shared. But she wouldn't think about that now. She was there for only one reason.

* * *

Dominic dashed into the house, tossed his things in the foyer, unbuttoned his shirt and raced past the living room. He called out to the woman sitting there and said, "I'm just going to change my shirt. I'll be right with you." Suddenly, something registered in his mind. He slid to a complete stop and backtracked to get a second look at the woman sitting on his couch.

He stood in the frame of the doorway with his shirt halfway unbuttoned and one collar sticking up. He didn't care. He vaguely noticed Sergeant come up and greet him and absently patted him on the head.

He felt as though someone had punched him in the gut. It had happened only twice in his lifetime. First when his father told him he was leaving his mother and ten years ago, when a young woman came up behind him and said, "Just because you're brilliant doesn't mean you have to annoy the professor."

He had spun around ready to snap back. He was tired of being told what he could and couldn't do. When he turned the first thing he saw was a really nice pair of breasts in a gray sweater. He quickly lifted his gaze and met startling, clear brown eyes.

No one had ever talked to him like that or boldly looked at him as their equal. He stood speechless, his tongue like lead in his mouth as he felt his heart racing.

"Just some friendly advice," she said. "I've heard he can make your life miserable." She walked away and he stood there feeling like he'd turned to marble.

She was halfway down the hall before he grabbed a classmate and pointed. "Who is that?"

He had a clear view of her but the other student, a few inches shorter, struggled to see. "Who?"

"The girl in the gray sweater."

"Oh, Brenda Everton. She's very nice. She helped me—"

"Thanks," Dominic interrupted, patting him on the shoulder. He raced after her, but lost her when she went outside. He had given up searching for her, then he saw her sitting on the grass with a large sketch pad. He punched his hand into his fist bursting with triumph, then walked up to her. He sat down beside her. "You think I'm brilliant?"

"Yes." She didn't turn to acknowledge him and spoke in a matter-of-fact way, without the hint of a compliment.

He glanced at the ground. He didn't know what to say to her and it was clear he didn't affect her the way she did him and that annoyed him. But he didn't leave. He wasn't leaving without a phone number. With effort he'd gotten her to talk and to open up about her drawing and he'd discussed his filmmaking aspirations. He felt as though they were connected on some cosmic plane; that an intricate bond existed between them.

Whatever she did to him that day had changed his entire focus. He'd married her six months later and his life had never been the same.

He felt that same cosmic shift now as if his life was about to take another direction. The woman sitting in his living room was not the Brenda he remembered and yet she was everything he knew she could be: beautiful, bold and dangerous to him. He welcomed the challenge. He walked toward her.

"You've decided not to change your shirt?" she asked.

"I've decided not to keep you waiting any longer." He couldn't take his eyes off her as though she were a sorceress who had bewitched him.

"Good." She stood. "I've been admiring your house. You have a great view." The back of her skirt revealed a high slit, giving him a nice view of her legs and emphasized the curve of her behind.

Dominic rolled up his sleeves, his voice deepening into huskiness when he noticed the seductive rose on her ankle. "Mine's better."

Brenda bent down and lifted her briefcase. The motion only improved his view. He was pleased to notice her fingers tremble. She wasn't as unaware of their attraction as she pretended to be. "Where are we meeting?" she asked.

He took her briefcase and rested it down. "The sunroom. Would you like a drink?" He continued buttoning up his shirt, wishing he didn't have to and took off his tie, keeping his gaze focused on her. He loved the way she'd put her hair back and let some fall against her face. He wanted to toy with those strands. He also wanted to toy with that red suit. He'd never seen her in red before, the color of passion and heat and he could feel his own pulse racing and he fought hard not to grab her and fulfill the fantasy quickly growing in his mind.

Dominic took a deep breath and shifted from one foot to the other, determined not to respond to her like some horny teenager, although that's how he felt. He would take this slow.

"No, I don't need a drink," she said. "I'd really like to talk to you."

"You'll get your chance," he said, placing his hand on the small of her back to lead her to the other room. "I'm yours all evening." *And all night if you want*.

She sent him a look of warning. "I only came here for business."

"Of course," he said, then smiled.

Chapter 6

The suit had been a mistake. Coming here had been an even bigger one. *She should have made her request over the phone,* Brenda silently scolded herself. She thought she could handle this and had been impressed when the housekeeper had shown her the elegant dinner table. But then the moments ticked away and memories began filling her mind. Then she heard his car and the front door slam, she heard his voice and saw him fly past. She was determined to keep a rein on her temper. Then he'd stopped and come back to look at her.

He hadn't looked at her like that in years, as if he

were slowly peeling away her clothes. No other man looked at her that way, and it reminded her of the first time she'd spoken to him…

He was one of the poorest grad students she'd ever seen. She wondered how he could afford college. He never noticed her or anyone. She never saw him with anyone else and doubted he had any friends. But she'd noticed him. The careless way he walked; his frayed shirts and one pair of sneakers that had the rubber sole coming loose. He seemed to have so much against him that something inside her wanted to see him succeed. She'd approached him in the corridor outside of the lecture hall. She wasn't nervous. She had seven brothers and was never afraid to approach a man, even a surly one.

"You're a smart guy, but you should be careful. Dr. Prentice could flunk you."

He spun around and she braced herself for a cutting remark, but didn't get one. He didn't even look at her at first and she wondered if she'd underestimated his temper. Then he lifted his gaze and eyes shining with brilliance and fierce independence blazed into hers igniting an attraction she didn't know she had. Her heart jolted and she felt her entire body grow hot.

She stumbled over her next few words. "It's because you challenge him and he doesn't take well to that and can be very vindictive. That's my observation."

He made a noncommittal sound deep in his throat, which she couldn't interpret and continued staring at her in that dark, magnetic way of his. "Just some friendly advice." She flashed a quick smile, then fled.

She felt like a coward but that didn't stop her from running. She could feel his gaze on her and ran until she knew he was gone. Once outside she had felt foolish and tried to convince herself that she'd made it all up, but her body knew differently and she still felt breathless. She decided to sketch and selected her favorite place to do so. She always carried a little sketchbook with her and felt herself relax as she focused on drawing a butterfly resting on a rock nearby.

"So you think I'm smart?"

She didn't dare turn around. She felt him sit beside her. The breathless feeling returned. She focused on her drawing because she didn't dare focus on him. "Yes."

He leaned in closer. The hairs on his arm brushed against her skin. "You're very good," he said.

"Thanks. I like to sketch. It keeps my mind clear. Sometimes I try to draw things from memory to see how much detail I can remember. Reminds me to be observant." *Dear God, she was rambling*. She snapped her sketchbook closed because it was clear he wasn't going to move and she'd have to. She needed to create distance.

"Do I make you nervous?"

"You make Dr. Prentice nervous."

"I can't help that."

"You can't be a filmmaker if you don't know how to work with people."

"How did you know about that?" he demanded.

"I saw your documentary. I would have missed it but my younger brother was visiting and watching TV and turned it on. I really liked it."

He shook his head in disbelief. "I didn't think anyone would watch it. I still got a D."

His unhappiness surprised her. She'd thought he would rally against such things as a professor's criticism. She didn't want anything or anyone to crush his spirit. She ruffled through her bag, then pulled out a class project that still brought her pain. "My professor gave me a D for this. I cried for days until I realized that he just hated me and not my work."

He held the illustration. "This is great."

"Thanks."

He traced the illustration with his forefinger. "And he made you cry?"

"I was devastated, but I got over it."

"What was his name again?" he asked the question in such a quiet, neutral voice she sent him an uneasy look. Then she looked at his hands, he gripped the paper without creasing it, but he held it so tightly that the veins on the back of his hands popped out. His anger surprised and concerned her. She gently covered his hand, amazed by the size and strength of it. "It doesn't matter now. I passed."

He didn't look at her, instead he stared at their hands. She quickly removed hers and stood.

"Where are you going?"

"I have to go to class."

"Can I call you?"

"Sure."

He called her the next day and they were married six months later. She stared at him now. There were no longer frayed shirts or bursts of insecurities, he was a self-made multimillionaire and knew it.

They sat in his enclosed sunroom, the crisp autumn wind beating against the window as the sign of the approaching winter. Brenda looked at the large table covered with a damask table cloth, candles and a large display of fresh flowers in the middle. It was an effortlessly romantic setting: the sound of the water, the soft lights of the city, and soothing classical music drifting in through speakers. She remembered when… No, Brenda caught herself. She was there on business, not pleasure.

But Dominic made that difficult. Throughout dinner—which consisted of smoked salmon, sweet potatoes, asparagus, sweet rolls and red wine—he refused to talk about why she was there. He was a great conversationalist and they talked about everything but that. After her favorite dessert, chocolate mousse, Brenda felt more relaxed and Dominic finally brought up the topic, while leading her into the family room.

"I'm happy you called me," he said taking a seat on a large sofa. "I was a little worried about you."

"You don't have to be." Brenda adjusted her skirt as she sat down in a side chair and faced him.

"Madeline left me a letter."

Brenda paused, surprised. "She did?"

He nodded. "Did she leave you one too?"

"Yes."

"What did yours say?"

"I'm not going to tell you."

He shrugged. "Fair enough, but after what happened did it make you want to change?"

"It made me think about my life."

"Now you're ready to have one."

"Oh, that's hilarious coming from you. How much time do you actually spend in this house?"

"I told you," he said slowly. "I've altered my priorities. I don't work as much as I used to."

"Really?" She glanced at his organizer on the side table next to him.

"Yes."

She held out her hand. "Let me see your schedule for next week."

"No."

"Why not? Do you have something to hide?"

He rubbed his nose, uncomfortable. "This month's a bit crowded."

"I knew you hadn't changed."

He opened his organizer and handed it to her. She glanced through it. "I'm surprised you have time to sleep."

"Yes, it looks crowded, but that's only because I'm not seeing anyone at the moment. I guarantee you, if I were, my schedule would look differently."

"I'm sure it would."

He let her sarcasm slide. "So what can I do for you?"

Brenda cleared her throat. She'd practiced what she would say, but oddly, she felt awkward. "I didn't get funding for phase two of my project and I need a loan."

"A loan?" he repeated.

"Yes, a loan. I had thought of you as an investor, but that would include too much paperwork and involvement."

He sat back, his gaze sharp. "And you just want my money, not me."

"It's more complicated than that. I—"

He folded his arms. "How much do you want?"

"About a million."

"I don't deal in 'abouts'. How much do you need?"

"One point five million."

"How do you plan to pay back this loan?"

She opened her briefcase. "I've sketched it all out here." Brenda spread several papers out on the glass center table, confident that he would be impressed.

Dominic glanced at the papers, then shook his head. "I'm not in the mood to read. Just tell me."

"But I have everything laid out. If you'd just—"

"Brenda, it's a simple question. If I have to go through four pages to find out the answer, it's a bad risk." He leaned forward. "I know you. You can be very straightforward when you want to be. But when you don't know an answer, you stall. You create complex replies. That may work with others, but it doesn't work with me." He traced the edge of the table, his tone unrelenting. "Now, I'm going to ask you again. How do you plan to pay back this loan?"

Brenda stared down at her carefully laid out illusion: the typed pages with all her projections. He was smart, she should have known better. She should have remembered she couldn't deceive him. "I don't know." She raised her gaze, determined. "But I will. You know my word is good."

He sat back. "Your word may be good, but I can't depend on your vows."

The words hit her like a slap, making her angry.

"Don't give me that. You wanted the divorce as much as I did."

He blinked, but didn't respond.

"Are you going to give me the loan or not?"

"No."

Brenda cooled her anger, quickly gathered her papers, then stood. "Okay."

"Sit down. I haven't finished yet."

"Then talk to your dog." She turned to leave.

"I said sit."

"I'm not staying to hear your explanation."

His gaze remained on her like a laser and each moment she defied him the laser burned hotter. He rarely shouted at anyone, and definitely not at her. He just became very quiet with all the calm of an approaching tornado.

She sat, reluctantly.

Dominic did not smile with triumph. Instead, he lowered his gaze and kept his voice soft. "I'm not going to loan you the money, I'm going to give it to you."

"Give it to me?"

"Yes, but I want you to do something for me in return."

"I knew there would be a catch," she said in disgust.

He got up and started to leave.

"No, wait," she said, realizing her error. "Okay, I'm listening."

He settled back in his chair. "I'm working on a book and I need an illustrator."

"Your publisher will hire one for you."

"I know that, but I want you."

She shook her head. "Impossible. I haven't illustrated in years."

"Is that a no?"

"It's a 'you're out of your mind.'"

"Okay." He stood up again and left.

Brenda jumped up and followed him.

"Dominic, be reasonable."

"I'm willing to give you over a million dollars for twenty illustrations and you're asking me to be reasonable? Are you afraid? Is that why you're turning me down?"

"I'm not afraid." She was *terrified*. She couldn't remember the last time she had had to work on a drawing assignment.

"Then what's holding you back?"

She couldn't admit weakness to him and besides, she needed the money. She took a deep breath, determined to think rationally, not emotionally. "What's the project?"

He went into another room, then returned with some papers. "This."

She stared at the outlined description. "This could take an entire year to complete. I don't have that kind of time to take away from my research."

"Yes, you do. Your research is progressing well. And that fellow you work with, Chuck, is a brilliant scientist and can take the lead. You have the lab and the researchers. It doesn't need your daily involvement anymore, you're basically just supervising so you have time to help me."

"Who's the publisher? What if they don't like my style?"

A sly grin touched his face. "You're afraid."

She stiffened. "No, I'm not."

He held out his hand. "Then we'll be working together."

"Maybe we should have a trial run first. I could produce a few samples and—"

He rested his hands on his hips. "It's all or nothing." He pinned her with an intense stare.

She hesitated. "There's one more thing."

"What?"

"Well, my water heater just busted."

"And you need money to replace it."

"Yes."

"Now that changes things," he said, thoughtful.

"Why?"

"Because that's a personal request."

She tilted her head to the side and folded her arms. "It's not that personal."

"If you want money for your water heater you have to invite me over for dinner."

"Why?"

"That's my condition. Take it or leave it."

"But I don't cook, you know that."

"You can order something."

"This doesn't make any sense to me. First you want illustrations and then dinner. Why?"

Dominic pulled her against his hard, solid body and covered her mouth with his. His mouth was even sweeter than she remembered. Her body shamelessly responded to being in his arms again. He always made her feel wicked and wild. But before she could completely lose control, he abruptly pulled away, his voice as unsteady as she felt. "That's why."

"You're not getting *that* as part of our partnership," she said, breathless.

"No, I expect to get *that* for free."

His arrogance infuriated her. She raised her fists to hit him in the chest, but he grabbed them before she struck him. "Go on and fight me, Brenda," he whispered. "Fight me long. Fight me hard, fight me with all your might until you're weak. Then when you surrender, I'll be ready."

"I'll never surrender to you."

"You want me." He kissed her fist, easing his leg between hers. "Don't think I don't feel it."

"It's just the fact that you're a man, not that it's you."

His jaw twitched and anger briefly darkened his eyes, then passed. "I'm going to forgive you for that, but watch your mouth because I know how to close it." He kissed her neck. "You smell good and feel even better. I'd take you to bed tonight if I knew you were ready. But you'd convince yourself it was all a mistake and regret it in the morning no matter how good it was. And you'd lie just to punish me."

She blinked at him as if she were bored. "May I go now?"

His gaze locked into hers and she could see him measuring how far he was going to push her, then he stepped back. "We start next week. You have a few days to prepare."

"For what?"

"The fact that I'm going to seduce you."

"You can try."

The corner of his mouth kicked up in a wicked grin. "You know me better than that, Brenda. I don't *try*. I succeed."

She wasn't scared, Brenda told herself on her drive home. That wasn't her problem. No, she wasn't scared, she was aroused. Dangerously so. But that had always been her weakness when it came to Dominic. However, this time she was determined to resist. She could handle him. And no matter what seductive ploy he used she would fight it.

As she changed her clothes, his kiss still lingered on her lips. If she licked them she was certain she could taste him. She was afraid that if she looked at her body she'd see where his hands had been as if he'd imprinted himself on her, not that she needed to see anything, her body remembered everything. Thank God she still had a working shower—cold water was all she needed.

Thomas stared at Dominic, stunned. He leaned on the desk. "Are you out of your mind?"

Dominic tossed his yo-yo in the air. "No, I've made my decision."

"You want to forgo the opportunity of a lifetime so you can write a book?"

He directed the yo-yo to the ground. "Yes."

"Okay, what about the other deal we discussed?"

Dominic caught his yo-yo in a quick decisive motion. "I'm saying no to that too."

Thomas took a deep breath. Dominic and his damn yo-yo. He could strangle him with it. But then again, the guy was making him rich so he couldn't do that. He had to reason with him. "But this is TV. This is the next level for you."

"TV is nothing new for me."

"This is the National Geographic channel and they

want you to be their technical advisor on a major new series."

"I'm not interested."

"You don't understand what this means. Think about the money."

"I have plenty of money."

"The prestige."

"I have that too. I've been on radio, TV, in magazines, newspapers, trade journals. I've traveled the world and met fascinating people. I've done a lot of things, but after doing them, I go home alone."

"Is that what you want? A woman? I can get you one. Hell, you can get one yourself, but if you're too busy I'll find one for you. Just tell me the type you like and she's yours."

"I found my type years ago and I plan to get her back."

"You mean Brenda?" he said with such disgust that Dominic sent him a look as powerful as a punch. He cleared his throat. "You know second chances are rare."

"But not impossible."

"Improbable."

"But not impossible," he repeated. "You should have seen her last night. She was amazing and she did it all for me. She doesn't know it yet, but she'll find out soon enough."

"I don't mean to poke holes in your theory, but have you considered that there could be someone else she's trying to impress?"

"There's nobody else." He paused, suddenly unsure. "If there is, he won't last long."

"She could just want your money."

"Brenda's not like that. It's as I told you. She's changed and I've changed and it's going to work out for the two of us. I'm going to get my wife back. And my first plan starts with fixing her water heater. I want you to handle that for me." He opened a drawer, then placed an ad from the newspaper on the table. "Make sure it's the best and I want it to be one of these. I want it installed immediately. See that it happens."

Thomas pasted on a smile. "You can trust me."

Thomas stuffed the ad in his pocket and swore as he walked to his car. He hated Brenda Everton. He had hated her ten years ago and he hated her even more now. Too much was at stake for her to get in his way again. Before, when Dominic was just getting started, she'd managed to confuse his priorities, making him feel guilty if he missed a couple dinners or their anniversary.

He'd been glad when she'd cut Dominic free by giving him a divorce. Finally, Dominic was all his and he'd worked with him to make him the success he was today. It was his effort that had got them there and he wouldn't allow Brenda to get in the way. She was messing with his plan. He was going to make Ayers Corporation even bigger than it was, and he couldn't have the president and CEO flake out on him now, not over a woman. He had to get Brenda out of the picture.

Thomas pulled out the ad and stared at the listed amount. Dominic was too generous. He'd get her the water heater, but it wouldn't cost this much.

He called a friend. "I have a job for you. I want it done quick and cheap."

Chapter 7

"Do you think this is a joke?" The voice on the phone was female and angry.

Brenda pulled the receiver from her ear and stared at it a moment, she'd had a long day and didn't want to deal with prank calls. She placed the phone against her ear and demanded, "Who is this?"

"Marci, and you haven't worn any of your new items to work."

Busted. "I did wear the outfit you suggested on my date."

"That was over a week ago."

"How do you know?"

"I told you we have spies."

"At least I wore it."

"That's not good enough. You wanted to see your life change, but you have to change too. I'm thinking of putting in a request to have some of your privileges revoked."

"What privileges?"

"You won't know about them if you don't get them."

"Now wait," Brenda said, feeling hurt. "Change takes time."

"You're wasting my time with your excuses. Tomorrow you're going to start dressing as the new Brenda. If you don't, you'll be sorry when you hear from me again." She hung up.

Brenda replaced the receiver, annoyed. Marci could have given her credit for at least wearing the suit. But she didn't want to get in trouble again. She didn't want to fail.

What am I supposed to wear to work? Brenda wondered as she stood looking at her closet. Never before had she seen so much color in her wardrobe. She wasn't against color. She liked color on flowers, cars, houses, but not on herself. When she was in art school, she wore primarily black despite the brilliant watercolors she loved to paint. She admired the other students who could casually mix and match. But with her height, she stood out enough; she didn't need or want to emphasize her presence.

Last week had been a hectic week and clothes hadn't been a priority, but at least she'd gotten her water heater fixed. Brenda frowned. There were too many choices and no Marci to help guide her. Brenda stepped back and took a deep breath. She would create a color-coded system matching all the items with each other.

I can do this. I don't want to hear from Marci again. Brenda worked into the evening, creating a color-coded fashion file. She translated her notes, detailing which color went with which basic item, such as a skirt, pants or jacket. Nothing in her wardrobe was left out, including accessories such as handbags, of which she only had two, belts, scarves, which she rarely wore, sweaters and shoes. She found shoes particularly challenging. While she had agreed to select several pairs with moderate heels, she wasn't sure she would feel comfortable wearing them.

Once she was finished, Brenda arranged the cards in a large file box. Although she was exhausted, she felt accomplished. No more anxiety. She didn't have to worry. She would always get an outfit right.

Her sense of accomplishment dwindled when she looked at the five leftover pieces of clothing on her bed. They were items Marci had *insisted* she needed: a backless silk halter top, a pair of brown leather straight-legged pants, a floor-length ball gown and a pink and black lace bra and panty set, which had made her blush when Marci handed it to her.

Brenda decided to put them in a large metal trunk she kept in her basement. It was unlikely she would wear any of them anyway. She had never worn anything like the backless halter top, and did not plan to start now. As for the leather pants, they reminded her of a girl she knew in college who only wore short leather skirts and tight leather pants, and probably hadn't kept them on very long.

The floor-length ball gown seemed like a trivial item, although it was gorgeous. She hadn't worn anything like it since attending her high school prom. Where would she wear something like that? Even when she was married to Dominic, their schedule had always been busy and they never attended any event where such an extravagant outfit would be needed. Last, but certainly not least, while she was not one to be prudish, the two-piece panty set verged on risqué. She'd really have to trust Mr. Ideal before she wore it for him.

For work the next day, Brenda carefully selected a dark blue straight skirt hitting just above the knee, a fitted long-sleeved light gray shirt touched off with a red leather belt, a pair of three-inch dark blue sling back shoes, and a hand-painted pastel silk scarf

An Important Message from the Publisher

Dear Reader,

Because you've chosen to read one of our fine novels, I'd like to say "thank you"! And, as a special way to say thank you, I'm offering to send you two more Kimani™ Romance novels and two surprise gifts – absolutely FREE! These books will keep it real with true-to-life African American characters that turn up the heat and sizzle with passion.

Please enjoy the free books and gifts with our compliments...

Linda Gill

Publisher, Kimani Press

Peel off Seal and Place Inside...

EDITOR'S
FREE GIFTS
SEAL
THANK YOU

THE EDITOR'S "THANK YOU" FREE GIFTS INCLUDE:

Two Kimani™ Romance Novels
Two exciting surprise gifts

YES! I have placed my
Editor's "thank you" Free Gifts
Seal in the space provided at
right. Please send me 2 FREE
books, and my 2 FREE Mystery
Gifts. I understand that I am
under no obligation to purchase
anything further, as explained on
the back of this card.

PLACE FREE GIFTS SEAL HERE

168 XDL EVGW

368 XDL EVJ9

FIRST NAME	LAST NAME

ADDRESS

APT.#	CITY

STATE/PROV.	ZIP/POSTAL CODE

Thank You!

DETACH AND MAIL CARD TODAY!

(K-ROM-09)

BUSINESS REPLY MAIL

FIRST-CLASS MAIL   PERMIT NO. 717   BUFFALO, NY

POSTAGE WILL BE PAID BY ADDRESSEE

THE READER SERVICE
3010 WALDEN AVE
PO BOX 1867
BUFFALO NY 14240-9952

NO POSTAGE
NECESSARY
IF MAILED
IN THE
UNITED STATES

draped around her shoulder. She wore her hair in a ponytail and put makeup on.

Brenda looked at herself. She looked and felt fantastic. Life was good. She had the money to fund her project and her water heater had been fixed. She hadn't heard from Dominic, but that was probably best, she'd been thinking about him more than she should. She needed the distance. It helped put everything into perspective.

"Wow," Chuck said when he saw her. Brenda stood at her bookshelf giving him a full view of her new look. He'd never seen her out of a lab coat. "What's the occasion?"

She shrugged and pushed a book back in place. "No special occasion. When I left Madeline's funeral, I realized that I need to live now, not later."

Sonya burst into the room. "I heard about it, but I had to see it for myself and prove they weren't lying." Sonya approached Brenda as though afraid the image before her was an apparition that would disappear. "I can't believe it. You're gorgeous. Have you ever modeled before? I'm sure you could model now. Older models are in now. Not that I'm saying you're old or anything."

"I understand."

"You don't even look like you. You look like you

should be standing on the edge of a mansion with a piña colada in one hand."

"Not quite."

"Or in a boardroom with a room full of men and a whip—I mean pointer—in one hand."

Brenda repressed a laugh. "Thank you." Someone knocked. She glanced at Chuck, then at Sonya amazed: she'd never been so popular before. "Come in."

Kendell entered. "I have a gift for you—" He stopped and stared at her.

"Yes?" she encouraged when he didn't speak.

He stepped back and looked at the sign on the door. "Sorry, I was looking for Dr. Everton."

"That would be me."

"Doesn't she look great?" Sonya said.

Kendell made a gurgling noise in his throat.

Brenda folded her arms. "You have something for me?"

He came out of his stupor. "Right. Yes, a gift card as a thank-you for your help." He held it out as though offering her roses.

She took it and rested it on her desk. "I was glad I could."

He flashed a teasing grin. "I'm sorry I can't ask you for any more favors."

"Why not?"

"My wife might get jealous."

Brenda raised her eyebrows in mock censure. "Careful, Dr. Baldwin."

"I saw her first," Chuck said.

"You're married."

"So are you."

Brenda raised her hands and laughed, flattered by the attention. "That's enough, you two. We came here to work and that's what I plan to do."

But she didn't get much of an opportunity. Her new look brought her a fleet of male admirers. She welcomed the attention, hoping her ideal man was hidden among them. In only one week she had gotten three offers of marriage from complete strangers, had her lunch and breakfast, which she usually ate in the cafeteria, paid for the entire week by an unknown admirer, and had two dozen roses delivered to her office by someone named Romeo.

Being practical, Brenda did not follow up on any of them. Her ideal man would not be so uncreative or secretive. He would be bold and speak to her directly. He would not send her flowers anonymously or propose marriage, based solely on lust. Lust was fine, but not for the long term. It had gotten her in trouble before. She'd know him once she met him.

A week later Chuck came to her office and asked, "Have you been able to secure the funding we will need?"

Brenda hesitated, she hadn't heard from Dominic but knew she could trust him. "Yes. I spoke to an individual willing to provide us with funding to complete the project."

"Who?"

"He prefers to remain anonymous." She didn't know if he did, but since it was up to her, he would.

"That's great, I can't wait to tell the team."

"Not just yet. I prefer to wait until I've signed the papers and the money is in the bank. By the way, as part of the funding, I added a new position so that you will have someone to help you. You have never complained about all the time you have put in and I am grateful for your dedication and commitment, but you have a family.

"With an assistant, you will be able to spend more time with them and you'll be in charge of hiring him or her."

He stared at her with hope. "Does this mean…?"

"Yes, you've been promoted."

"I knew today was my lucky day. Now everything is perfect. There's nothing to worry about." He left.

But he was wrong. Everything wasn't perfect. Another week passed and she still hadn't heard from Dominic. Brenda reminded herself that he wouldn't let her down, but as the days passed she started to worry. What if he'd forgotten his promise?

What if he didn't realize how desperate she was? What about the illustrations she was supposed to do for him? Part of her had looked forward to the project. Had it just been a ploy? She hated being disappointed.

Brenda thought about buying another package of cigarettes, then thought of something better: work. Work always kept her mind occupied. It had saved her sanity through her divorce and it would save her now. She wasn't like Madeline, she assured herself. She wasn't depressed and she'd never take her own life. But she wouldn't be put on hold either, not for a man and definitely not for Dominic. Waiting patiently was never a strong trait of hers. She would work hard and when she worked hard she expected others to do the same.

"I need the final report next week," she told Chuck a few days later. "Will you be able to complete it by then?" She did not look up from her desk so she couldn't see his nod and the odd way he looked at her. "Yes," he said.

"Can you please schedule a meeting for me with Dr. Ramsey for Thursday, and make an appointment with the scientific supply company in Tacoma? I'd like you and me to go and look for some new equipment."

"Brenda?" Chuck said.

"Yes."

"We have a problem."

That caught her attention and she looked at him. "What is it?"

"You."

She set her pen down. "Me?"

"We'd all hoped that the new look meant you had a new view of life, but you're working harder than before."

"No, I'm not," she said, insulted. "I'm excited about all we've been able to accomplish."

Chuck stared at her, seeing through her lie. "I care about you. What's wrong?"

"Nothing."

"You haven't been yourself since Madeline's death."

She took a deep breath before her temper got the better of her. "This has nothing to do with Madeline. So she died—that was her choice. I'm not like her. We were friends, not twins. I'm not prone to the same depressed disposition she was prone to. I wish people would leave me alone."

"Something's bothering you and it's affecting the project."

"I thought the project was progressing well."

"The project is, but we're not. The team's morale is low. You have been going non-stop and pushing us non-stop too. You want this and that, you are going here and there, you'll burn out. But we will probably burn out before you do."

"Chuck—"

"Take a week off."

Brenda stared at him, stunned. "What?"

"Take the week off."

Brenda sat speechless. Who was he to talk to her like that? She was the boss and he was the man who crumbled in a crisis. She opened her mouth to protest, then realized the courage it took for him to stand up to her. She shrugged, resigned. She didn't want to do anything to jeopardize the project at this stage. "Fine."

His tone softened. "You need it."

Although she knew he cared, she felt betrayed and didn't look at him when she left.

Chapter 8

She didn't remember his name and she didn't care anymore. Two days ago she had been certain she'd finally met Mr. Right, but now she knew she hadn't. Brenda sat in Sam's Coffee House staring at the man in front of her, trying not to fall asleep. She'd met him in a bookstore and he'd seemed interesting when he'd suggested they have coffee together. Unfortunately, the coffee wasn't strong enough to keep her awake.

Over the last few days she'd learned a lot about herself. She didn't like the bar scene, concerts were too long, cocktails too shallow and the Internet too impersonal. At least at a bookstore she'd meet someone intelligent—or so she thought.

What's His Name was tall, clever, good looking in a clean cut sort of way, and about as exciting as dry wheat toast.

Brenda had hoped he would be a nice diversion. She'd figured coffee could lead to lunch, which could lead to dinner, which could eventually lead to breakfast. Now she wished she could just lead him to the door. Methods of escape filled her imagination. She glanced around, wondering if she could find a familiar face and pretend that she had to speak with them.

Her gaze fell on Franklin as he stood at the counter. She quickly glanced away with a tiny shiver. Anyone but him. However, after several minutes of desperately searching for an alternative, she knew she had no other choice and inwardly groaned, resigned. He'd have to be her rescuer. She watched him with his coffee and biscotti and saw him stuff his change into his jacket pocket. In a few seconds he would leave. This was her only chance.

Brenda jumped up. "I'm sorry," she said to her companion. "There's someone I have to speak to." She pointed to Franklin. "It's important. Great to see you again. Talk to you soon." She rushed over to Franklin. "Oh there you are. I've been looking for you."

Franklin looked at her, confused. "What?"

To her horror What's His Name followed her
and said, "Do you really have to leave so soon? I
could wait."

"No." She slid her arm through Franklin's,
ignoring his startled look. "We have a big complicated project to discuss. I'm very sorry to leave you
like this."

He smiled with understanding. "I'll see you around."

Not if I'm hiding. "Yes."

She seized Franklin's arm and dragged him toward
the door. "Don't ask questions," she said in a low
voice. "Just keep walking." She raised her voice so
the other man could hear. "Now what was it that we
needed to discuss?"

Franklin went along and followed her outside, then
said, "What was that all about?"

She released her grasp. "An error in judgment."

"Have you thought about my question?"

"It's still no."

The man came out. "I forgot to ask you for your
phone number."

Brenda grabbed Franklin's arm again and smiled.
"Umm…I'm in the process of having it changed."

He handed her his card. "Perhaps we could get
together sometime."

She glanced down at it, her mind searching for an

excuse. At least she now remembered his name: Wallace.

"Well…"

"That's not possible," a cool, male voice cut in.

They spun around. Dominic stood facing them.

"Why not?" Wallace asked, affronted.

Dominic approached them. He looked casual, but Brenda saw the darkness in his eyes. Fury lurked behind his calm demeanor and he looked very much the avenging outlaw. "Because she's with me."

Wallace sent her an accusatory look. "You didn't tell me you were seeing anyone."

"Because I'm not," she said shooting Dominic a fierce glare. He had no right to come and claim her like this.

Dominic hooked his fingers in the belt hooks of his jeans. "You are now."

"This is none of your business, Ayers," Franklin said, putting a possessive hand on Brenda's. She resisted the urge to yank it away.

Dominic noticed the hands and his gaze darkened to onyx. "But it is."

Brenda shook her head, alarmed and exasperated. Things could get ugly if she wasn't careful. "Dominic, you can't come here and think you can—"

He ignored her, his gaze fixed on Franklin. "Take your hand off her."

Franklin stroked her hand. "She doesn't seem to mind where it is."

Dominic made a quick, dangerous move forward. Brenda stopped him with her free hand, he felt like solid rock. "This is ridiculous." She pulled free from Franklin. "I'm going home." She walked to her car.

The three men followed.

Wallace said, "You didn't give me your number."

Franklin said, "I still want you to think things over."

Dominic cut in front of her. "I want to talk to you."

She halted and glared up at him. Four weeks of waiting to hear from him made her tone extra vitriolic. "I don't want to talk to you." She then turned to Franklin. "And I've told you my answer is no." She finally looked at Wallace. "Thank you for the coffee, but I've decided to stop seeing men for a while."

Brenda then got in her car and drove off. It took her only a couple miles to realize she was being followed. In the dim light she couldn't see the driver, but she knew it was Dominic. He was trying to intimidate her, but she wouldn't let him. The best way to handle him was to ignore him.

She pulled into her driveway and parked, then walked inside her house. She changed into something comfortable, ate some leftovers, then looked through the window to check her driveway. His car still sat there like a large, dark presence. She wrote some bills, watched a sitcom and then checked outside again. The car hadn't moved. Fueled by anger, and knowing that he would stubbornly sit in the cold all night until she let him in, Brenda grabbed her jacket, marched up to the car and pounded on the window. It slowly rolled down.

"Get in the house," she ordered, then spun away.

She could hear the grin in his voice when he said, "Thought you'd never ask."

Once inside Dominic casually removed his coat, then sat in the living room. "Nice place."

Brenda didn't care for compliments. "What are you doing here?"

"I wanted to make sure you made it home safely."

"You wanted to make sure I made it home alone."

He nodded. "That too."

She sat across from him and crossed her legs. She watched his gaze dip to her legs and she inwardly grinned. *Go ahead and look at what you'll never get.* She had forgotten that she was wearing the sensual lounge wear Marci had selected.

"You don't need to wait to have a man to wear these," Marci had said. "Whenever you're stressed, or just want to enjoy and acknowledge your woman-hood, wear it." She was glad she had, although she hadn't expected company, and didn't mind him seeing it. She didn't try to cover up how the front dipped low showing her cleavage or how it fell away from her thigh.

But his gaze didn't waver and soon became as intimate as a caress. Brenda decided to cover her thigh and fold her arms over her chest. "What do you want?"

His smoldering gaze left her body and met her eyes. "So this is the greeting I get on my return? Your hand on Franklin's arm while flirting with another man?"

"My activities are none of your business."

"You know it's my business because you know my intentions."

"Your intentions mean nothing to me."

"You don't believe a man can change?"

"A man can try, but whether he is successful or not will take time to figure out."

"So you see no hope for me?" he said in disbelief.

"What's changed? You're just like before."

"I said I'd get back to you."

"Four weeks later?" Her voice cracked. "You always kept me waiting. You always gave all your attention to other people and I got what was left over. I want a man who will give me all of his attention."

"You'd grow bored with a man who fawned all over you."

"I'd have fun finding out."

"Then divorce him when he's not up to standard."

"We divorced each other. You did it with your travel

and long nights. I did it with papers. I made it official so our marriage wasn't a complete mockery."

"Our marriage was real," he shouted. "You just didn't think it was perfect enough. It didn't fit your systematic analysis so it was a project you decided to abandon."

"Abandon? Half the time you didn't even know I was there."

"I've admitted I wasn't always there for you, but I've told you I've changed."

"How have you changed? A promise of seduction and then four weeks of nothing. Suddenly you show up again and expect me to be there for you."

"I didn't realize you hated me this much," he said with pain.

"I don't hate you," she said, surprised he used such a harsh word.

"Then what about the postcards? Didn't they mean anything to you?"

"What postcards?"

"The ones I sent you every week. I also e-mailed the manuscript for the book so we could discuss which illustrations would work when I returned."

She sat back bewildered. "I don't know what you're talking about. I didn't receive anything."

"But I—" He shook his head with frustration. "I don't understand."

Brenda felt her anger die as she realized the magnitude of his words. "You sent me something every week?"

"Yes."

"What did you say?"

He shrugged and looked a little embarrassed. "They were just a few lines. Nothing interesting."

"Tell me anyway."

"Okay." He stared at the ground. "Um…one said 'This place has more rain than Seattle, hope you're keeping dry.'" He rubbed the back of his neck and glanced at her, unsure.

"Go on," she urged.

"Another said how boring my meeting was and how much I looked forward to working with you. The last one said 'Coming home.'" He shook his head. "I mean 'Coming back soon. Looking forward to talking to you.'"

"I'm sorry I didn't receive them," Brenda said softly. She remembered that he used to do that at the beginning of their marriage, although they were rarely apart back then. Whenever he traveled he sent a postcard, but as the years passed they stopped coming, and he was away most of the time.

"And nobody called you?" Dominic asked, still amazed.

She shook her head.

"It doesn't make sense. It's not like Thomas not to follow instructions. Did you get the water heater installed?"

"Yes, thank you."

"It must have been a misunderstanding. I specifically told him that I wanted you to know where I was and what I was up to."

She smiled. "That was nice of you."

"I wasn't trying to be nice." He sat beside her. "I told you things will be different this time." Dominic pulled her to him and kissed her. His kiss reminded her of powdered sugar. She'd had some on her lips the first time they'd kissed and he'd used it as an excuse, he didn't need one after that. She welcomed his kiss as the desert sands welcome a breeze. His lips reminded her of warm Hawaiian beaches where they'd celebrated their honeymoon, late night showers, early morning quickies and tangled sheets.

There was something both safe and familiar yet dangerous and strange about him. He'd once been her husband but three years had made them strangers.

She pushed him away, his kiss burning her lips and her heart beating like thunder. She stood. "No, we can't do this again."

He stood too. "Do what again? Feel? You know enough about science to know that certain elements are drawn to each other because they have to be together."

"We are not single-cell organisms. We are rational human beings given the privilege of choice and I won't do this again." She turned away.

He came up behind her and whispered, "Why resist what your body tells you is right?" His voice was warm against her neck, making her skin prickle with pleasure. "You know that no other man makes you feel this way."

She faced him determined to resist what her body told her was right. "You possessed me once, but you will not do so again."

"You're already mine." He playfully tapped her nose. "Try not to think about me tonight."

She brushed his finger away. "I'll think of you as a warning never to trust my heart again."

He lowered his gaze. "I may have broken your heart." He lifted his gaze. "But you're the one who ripped it out and crushed it with your sense of right and wrong and unyielding judgment. I'm going to give you back your heart and make you whole again."

"Why don't you just give me yours?"

His gaze clung to hers. "Because I'd never trust you with it."

"No, you never did."

His face eased into an indulgent smile. "You can't hurt me, Brenda, and you won't get rid of me this time."

"I know. I didn't ask for your money without knowing you'd be a technicality."

His smile became devious. "It's not wise to make me angry when I haven't given you any money yet."

"Then go ahead. Don't give it to me, it will only confirm the ruthless side of your nature I know exists. Do I need your money? Yes. Does that make me vulnerable? Yes. Will I allow you to use that vulnerability to control and humiliate me? No."

He stared at her amazed. "You think I want to humiliate you?"

"You've never forgiven me for divorcing you. Your pride took a direct hit. I know you're trying to punish me for that."

He lowered his voice in pity. "How sad. I thought your new look meant something but you haven't changed at all. You're still fighting battles that don't need to be fought. Have you ever thought, just for once, that I didn't want a divorce because marriage meant something to me? And that I'm here now because I want you back."

"I won't come back."

"Then we'll go forward. This is our second chance and I'm going to seize it and one day when you open your eyes you will too." He grabbed his jacket and headed for the door. "I'll have the money deposited into your account and I will send you the manuscript and talk to you later."

"Next month perhaps?"

He pulled her to him and smothered her mouth with a kiss that left her breathless. When he drew away his voice shook from a barely controlled emotion she couldn't understand. "Remember that and don't let me see your hand on Franklin's arm again." He slammed the door.

Anger radiated through his calm demeanor as Dominic returned to his car. He'd returned to the city looking forward to seeing Brenda again. He hadn't expected her to fall into his arms, but he definitely hadn't been prepared to see her hand on Franklin's arm as she flashed a coy smile at another man. He had struggled hard to stop the urge to knock the two men's heads together.

Brenda was his. He hadn't sent her postcards and his manuscript just so she could toy with him. He'd never be anyone's toy. He'd followed her home because he wasn't going to allow her to dismiss him as she had the others. Sitting in the car only let his anger grow, but it warmed him as the cold air seeped in. When she'd finally invited him inside he was ready to unleash his fury, only to be met with her own fury. And in an instant his anger turned into disbelief. She hadn't received any of his mail.

Sergeant greeted him when Dominic made it home that evening.

"Oh, you're back," Sheila said when she saw him. "I made you your favorite."

He patted his dog. "I'm not hungry," he snapped, then saw her face fall and softened his tone. "Thanks. I'll eat it later."

He went into his bedroom and sat on the bed without turning on the lights. Sergeant sat and stared up at him. "I'm all right," Dominic told the dog, stroking its head. "Just disappointed." He'd driven straight from the airport to Brenda's office, eager to see how much leeway he'd made with her. When Chuck told him she'd taken time off, he'd been disappointed because he'd told her when he was returning. Seeing her outside the coffee shop had been an accident, but then again maybe it was meant to be.

He looked at the bright red letters of his clock. He waited until late before he called Thomas.

The ringing phone startled Thomas out of bed. He groped for it in the blackness of early morning, then picked it up. "Hello?"

"What happened?" a dark voice said over the line.

Thomas instantly knew whom it belonged to. "What do you mean?"

"Brenda didn't know I was away. I thought I told you to tell her."

He could feel Natalie waking up beside him and lowered his voice. "I did tell her."

"But she said you didn't."

"Look, who are you going to believe? A bitter ex-wife or me? Your cousin and manager? Have I ever let you down? She probably lied just to put you on your guard." Silence greeted him. "Dominic?" he said, wondering if the phone had gone dead.

"Brenda doesn't lie," he said, causing goose bumps to form on Thomas's arm.

Thomas swallowed and turned on the lights, blinking against the shine. Wrong strategy. He wouldn't attack her character. He had to think fast and come up with another reason. "Maybe she just forgot. It's been a busy week and it was a short conversation." He switched the topic, hoping to distract Dominic. "How does she like the water heater?"

"She's very pleased."

"See? I told you I'd come through for you. It was just a little mix up."

"And it won't happen again?"

"No."

"Hmm." Dominic paused, then said, "How's the studio coming?"

"The studio is fine. I've found a great location for her."

"Good." The line went dead.

Thomas hung up, then fell back on the pillow.

Natalie sat up. "What was that about?"

"Dominic was confused about something."

"What?"

"Just something," he snapped. "It doesn't matter now."

"He asked about the studio space?" Natalie asked unfazed by his irritation.

"That's right."

"Where?"

"What do you care?"

"I'm just curious," she said in a small voice.

He saw no harm in telling her and filled her in on where it was located.

"You can't put her there," she said horrified. "That place is a dump."

He sat up and shrugged. "She'll get used to it. Artists like places like that."

"She'll blame Dominic. And he'll blame you."

"No, he won't. I'll tell him that's all I could find on such a short notice."

"Thomas—"

"I know what I'm doing," he said with a smug smile. "I've done it before."

"But—"

"Are you his manager or what? I'm the one who's gotten him this far. You got your job because of me.

Don't fool yourself into thinking you mean more than that. We both know that before me you were only qualified in how to spend your father's money. Don't put your pretty nose where it doesn't belong. Brenda's a gold digger."

"I don't think she's a gold digger."

"She's not good for him and Dominic needs to see that. I'm helping to make his vision clear." Thomas turned off the light and fell back to sleep.

Natalie stared at the shadows on the wall.

Chapter 9

"Cooking lessons!" Brenda read her instructions again: *Schedule an appointment with Rania for a special cooking session.* She set the paper down. She hated cooking. Why would she need to take lessons? If this was going to be the way to finding her ideal man, she was beginning to doubt the Society's claim of a guarantee. Her lack of cooking skills was known to her family and Dominic had never tasted it. She'd loved him too much to put him through that agony.

Perhaps the Society could work miracles, things were going well so far. She'd gotten men's attention, if this would improve her odds, she was up for the challenge. So she made an appointment.

Rania arrived on time that Saturday. Brenda didn't know whom she'd expected to arrive, but it wasn't a striking, full-figured dark-skinned woman in a cashmere coat and high heels with her arms filled with groceries.

"Put these items in your refrigerator right away," she said, handing Brenda two grocery bags. She followed Brenda inside, then stopped and stared once she entered the kitchen. "Oh my."

Brenda rested the bags on the counter. "What?"

"This looks like a science lab."

Brenda took it as a compliment. She took pride in her kitchen, although she never used it to cook in. It was orderly and immaculate, a masterpiece in design. All of the appliances were stainless steel, she had a granite countertop, a marble cutting block and a kitchen island. The herbs and spices sat lined up in neat rows, each one clearly labeled.

Rania opened the cupboard. "It's obvious you don't cook."

"How do you know?"

"Easy. Hand me the salt."

"Salt? I don't have salt."

"How about the flour?"

"No."

"Cooking spray?"

"No."

"How about a skillet?"

"Okay, you've made your point. I didn't know I was supposed to have those items. But, I can go to the store and get them."

Rania began unloading the bag. "You won't need to do that, Brenda. I came fully prepared. Do you have an apron?"

"Yes. Actually, I have a total of ten."

"Ten? Why ten?"

"It's a little family joke. They love the irony of someone like me having an apron. I'll get one for each of us." Brenda reappeared with two brand-new aprons. "Here, you can have this one. I like the one with the big pockets. And here's a box of latex gloves." She rested it on the counter.

Rania frowned. "Why do we need latex gloves?"

"One of the things I hate about cooking is touching raw meat. I know that sounds odd for a scientist, but that's the way I am. And I hate getting flour stuck under my fingernails. So whenever I cook, which is basically never, I always wear gloves."

Rania watched in amazement as Brenda carefully put on her gloves, as though preparing for a dissection. Rania sighed, then put on her apron. "Cooking is like chemistry. Simply science. That's why I'm sure once you know the basics you'll enjoy it.

"I don't intend to turn you into a chef, but the old adage, *the way to a man's heart is through his stomach,* holds more truth than we would like to think. I am going to show you how to prepare one complete meal including dessert, and I promise you, by the end of the day, you will be able to prepare it yourself." Rania briefly went over the basics, then pulled out three large laminated picture cards and placed them on the counter.

"Here are the recipes with clear instructions. If you follow them step-by-step, nothing will go wrong."

Great. Brenda thought. *Science she understood.* Before beginning any of the recipes Brenda read each one, then organized each ingredient in groups on the cooking island. She used a yellow highlighter to emphasize the measurements.

She pointed at one instruction. "What's this?"

Rania looked. "A pinch of salt."

"What exactly is a pinch?"

"It's small."

"I don't understand. What is the unit of measurement a pinch of salt should be? Is it like grams?"

Rania grabbed a pinch and put it in the bowl. "It's like that."

"Oh. Could you show me again?"

Rania took a deep breath. "No. We're making a basic dish. Shepherd's pie, a simple recipe that consists of a layer of browned ground beef and a layer of mashed potatoes on top, baked in the oven for approximately one hour at 350 degrees."

"Approximately? Does that mean less than one hour or more than one hour?"

"It means approximately."

"You cannot set the oven timer on approximately. It's either an hour or it's not."

Rania rubbed her forehead as though she had a headache. "It's an hour."

The session went downhill from there. Brenda burnt the beef, setting off the fire alarm; cut herself while peeling potatoes; washed the vegetables for nearly five minutes, then cut them into uniform, bite-sized pieces; demanded to know the difference among vegetable oil, canola oil, olive oil, corn oil, and sesame oil and then inspected each strawberry to be used in the dessert, throwing out any that looked bruised or defective.

Rania threw up her hands. "Stop!"

"What?"

"The perfectionism. The questions. It has to stop."

"What questions?"

Rania mimicked Brenda's voice: "'How small should the potatoes be cut? Half an inch or one inch in size?' 'Are you sure this is the right kind of butter to use?' 'What if I don't mash the potatoes correctly?' 'What does non-hydrogenated oil mean?'"

Brenda felt her face grow warm. "I just want to understand."

"You do understand. You're afraid of making a mistake and that's impossible. Mistakes are part of learning. You're going to do this quickly."

Brenda froze. She never did new things quickly. She hated the prospect of failing at something. Growing up, she had succeeded at everything she had ever done. She had been the valedictorian at her high school, was on the Dean's list throughout college and upon graduation had won a highly competitive international scholarship to study abroad for a year in London in a prestigious science lab.

But Rania rushed her through the rest of the session and in the end the meal didn't look as expected. Fortunately, it tasted fine. Both Brenda and Rania ate it, surprised.

"Wow," Brenda said with renewed confidence. "I would never have thought of making a dish like this," she said, taking a second helping of the pie. "When I go to visit my mother, I'll surprise her by making this."

"And others," Rania said. "Try to experiment. Remember it's not fatal to make mistakes."

The next day Dominic's manuscript arrived in her e-mail and she printed it out. She started reading, planning on just skimming a few pages, then getting to her laundry, but the depth and passion of his prose captivated her.

She finished the book and set it aside, amazed. He always told her how he envied her ability to draw, claiming he couldn't draw a stick figure, but he could write. It was the same skill that kept people entranced around the world. She knew this book, like his others, would be a bestseller.

She still had his first one. He'd dedicated it to her and signed it "With love." She hadn't looked at it in years, wondering when she'd be able to without feeling any pain. She lifted the manuscript again and ran her hand over his name, remembering his first effort at writing a book. She'd come home from teaching and found him sitting in front of the computer.

"So how is it coming?" she asked.

He glumly pointed to the screen. She peered over his shoulder and saw one sentence. "I can write papers, articles and lectures, but I don't know how to write a book," he said.

She rested her hands on his shoulder and kissed him on the cheek. "You don't have to. Just think of it as a presentation."

He shook his head. "It's not the same."

"It is the same." She gently shoved him from his seat. "Move."

"Why?"

"Because you're going to dictate." He reluctantly stood and Brenda took his seat and flexed her fingers. "Okay, begin."

He folded his arms, unimpressed. "This is not going to work."

"Yes it will. Tell me about…" She searched her mind, then gave him a subject.

At first his words were dull, then as he warmed to the topic they became interesting and fresh. Soon he didn't need her anymore. And over the following months she learned to fall asleep to the sound of the keyboard.

Then one evening he crawled in bed beside her and kissed the back of her neck. "I'm done."

She turned to him. "Really?"

He drew down the strap of her nightgown with intimate slowness. "Yes, really." He placed a feather-light kiss on her shoulder. "All thanks to you."

"I can't take all the credit," she said trying to sound rational, although his mouth and fingers made her feel anything but.

He drew down the other strap with equal deliberation. "You can take most of it."

"You did all the hard work." She licked her lips and watched him uncertain as he unbuttoned his shirt. "Dominic, what are you doing?"

He tossed his shirt aside and stared at her with innocence. "I'm getting ready for bed."

"You don't look like you're ready to sleep."

He unbuttoned his trousers. "I'm not. I'm planning to thank you."

"You don't need to thank me this much. You've worked very hard and I'm sure this book will be a hit."

He took off his trousers and tossed them aside also. "I don't care as long as you like it."

"I'll like it. I always like what you do."

He began to smile.

Brenda noticed the sensuous gleam in his eyes and shook her head. "Dominic, I have work tomorrow."

"No, you don't. You're not going in."

A knowing grin touched her mouth. "I'm not?"

"No, you're calling in sick."

"Why?"

"Because I'm going to keep you up all night." He pulled down her nightgown. "And then I'm going to cook you breakfast and make love to you until lunch."

"Then you'll cook lunch?"

"No, we'll order in." He leaned toward her.

She held him back. "Tempting, but I have lots of work to do tomorrow. Wait until the weekend."

"I don't want to."

"You have to." Brenda pulled up her nightgown, jumped out of bed and headed for the door. "I'm sleeping in the guest room."

Dominic leaped up and wrapped an arm around

her waist, pulling her up against him. "You're not going anywhere."

"We can't afford to lose work hours and—"

He spun her around. "Don't worry about the money."

She sighed with helpless frustration. "Dominic—"

"One day I'm going to make so much money you won't have to teach anymore. You'll do all the research you want."

"I don't mind teaching."

"You hate it."

She shrugged. "It pays the bills."

His jaw tensed and his gaze grew cool. "You don't believe that I can—"

She covered his mouth with her hand. His expression may have frightened someone else, but she knew him too well to ever fear him. He'd only looked at her like that once before when he'd discussed his mother and his terrible home life with her. She stared at him determined to erase that look from his face. "I believe that you can accomplish anything you want. I know you haven't even reached all that you're going to." She saw his gaze soften and smiled. She removed her hand, then kissed him. "Now good night." She turned to leave.

"I knew it was a brilliant idea."

She stopped. "What?"

"Marrying you. One day you'll feel the same."

"I already do."

"Then spend the night with me and let me take care of tomorrow. Trust me."

Brenda bit her lip, briefly shut her eyes then looked at him feeling all of her resolve melt away. She removed her nightgown and let it fall to the ground. "I do."

Dominic swung her into his arms and carried her to the bed. He gently eased her down on it before covering her body with his. The warmth of his hard flesh pressed against her sent a pure and explosive sense of desire cascading over her. Soon she no longer wanted to talk. She was consumed with the primitive need to feel him inside her; to be one with him. Within moments passion, desire, promises, love surrounded them as strong and unrelenting as a tropical storm. And when the fierceness of the storm threatened to ease, Brenda looked at Dominic and whispered, "Did you really mean what you said?"

"About what?"

"Making love to me all night until breakfast?"

Dominic didn't reply with words. However, he used his mouth to give her his answer.

The phone rang, jarring Brenda out of the past and forcing her back to the present. "Hello?"

"Did you like it?" Dominic asked.

The sound of his voice made her body grow hot; for a moment the past mingled with the present as she tried to erase the intimate memory she'd indulged in. She took a deep, steadying breath. "It's very good."

"You used to think my work was excellent."

"Yes." *I used to think everything about you was excellent.* She undid the button on her blouse, then tugged on it to cool herself. "You don't need my praise anymore—you have plenty of other people ready to stroke your ego."

"That's not why I asked you. I've always valued your opinion. You know that."

His honesty touched her. "I'm honored to be a part of this book. I know it's going to be a hit."

"Good. I'm ready to get started. I sent you an e-mail. I want us to meet Saturday."

"Okay. See you then."

That Saturday Brenda stared at her closet and realized she hadn't worn her second pair of stockings yet. She'd tried her first pair on Dominic, why not the second? She put on a pair of striped gray stockings, which felt heavenly and added a bit of danger to her legs, then selected a soft lime-green cashmere sweater dress.

At first she tried on a pair of cranberry-red flats, but they didn't work with the stockings or the dress. Instead they looked festive and made her look like a holiday decoration that only needed tinsel. She exchanged the shoes for a more subdued pair of two inch dark brown pumps.

She took a final look. Practical and sexy, but not over the top. Fitted but not too tight, and the green shade complimented both her figure and skin tone.

Brenda arrived early at their meeting place. She spent most of the time in the retail store next door looking at the display case filled with hand blown pottery. She lost track of time as her artistic nature took hold and she didn't mind late autumn's chilly air. She loved this part of the town, but hadn't been there in years. Her research project used up two hundred percent of her time. Over the years the area had changed considerably and was now the hub of the visual art scene in Seattle.

Most of the buildings had been renovated into artists' lofts or private, high-priced condominiums and apartments. Many years back, while attending a street festival in the area with Madeline, they had taken the opportunity to visit with some of the artists. One man stood out with large glasses and a selection of garish, hand-painted ties. They'd bought one for Dominic and begun their "ugly" tie tradition.

Brenda returned to the location Dominic had sent her. The building was a stately old brick structure right on the waterfront. For a moment, Brenda remembered the hours she had spent working on an oil painting, or completing a watercolor. During college, her favorite pastime had been sketching the many beautiful scenes Seattle provided. It wasn't called the Emerald City without justification. No matter what the season was, the majestic evergreens provided breathtaking views of the mountains and framed the waterways that surrounded the city. And she remembered her first studio, a room Dominic had transformed in their two-bedroom apartment.

Unfortunately, when they moved to their house, her priorities had changed by then and the paints and easel had been exchanged for a desk, pens and a microscope.

"Sorry I'm late," Dominic said, his breath coming out in white puffs.

"That's all right." She had seen him running toward her.

He paused as though he'd expected her to be angry and didn't know what to do because she wasn't. She saved him by saying, "I'm cold."

He took her hand. "Then let's go inside."

Chapter 10

Something was different. He didn't know what it was, but he could feel it. Dominic kept moving forward, although his mind was in chaos. He'd been prepared for a snide or sarcastic comment about his being late or for Brenda to yank her hand away from his, but she hadn't done anything. At last he was making progress. *The studio better be good or he'd serve Thomas to the wolves.*

He put the key in the door and opened it. He scanned the room, then he looked at Brenda. Her response was all that mattered.

She shook her head. "It's too big."

His hopes fell. "You don't like it?"

She grinned. "I didn't say that."

All his tension eased. He watched her take off her coat and hang it on the coatrack. She said something, but he didn't hear her. He couldn't believe what she was wearing; he noticed where the zipper was and knew that in one quick motion, he could have her out of it.

"Dominic?"

He blinked. "Huh?"

"This place must cost you a fortune to rent."

Rent? He'd bought it for her, but she'd discover that later. "You're working on my book and I always take care of anyone working for me." He meant to goad her by hinting that she was his employee, but she didn't take the bait. Yes, something was definitely different.

Brenda knew Dominic expected her to argue, but she wouldn't. Instead she noticed the rug and lighting and the sofa bed. He'd remembered how she used to work late at night into the early morning and had a habit of falling asleep in her studio. No, she wouldn't argue with him. She'd come determined to make a decision and he'd help her make it.

She looked out the window at the ripple of waves skidding across the lake. Soon she would return home and it would be another evening with a TV dinner and a sitcom. She thought of Madeline and the

Society's oath. She didn't have to find her ideal man right away. There would be no harm in them being together, at least through the empty winter months. It would be fun. They'd always had fun together. And incredible sex. It was the marriage that had been a disaster.

Dominic was a superb lover, unlike her two former boyfriends. They would always brag that they knew how to please any woman, before even taking off their clothes. Dominic knew the art of making love to a woman. Each and every encounter was an experience that stayed with her for days. His approach to lovemaking was enjoyable and uncensored, and always done playfully, unlike one boyfriend who approached sex like a mechanic working on a car. Every time they made love she wondered if he'd read an instruction manual:

First, pull the woman close to you and kiss the lips, then take your mouth down her neck and stop at the breasts. Caress them with your hands for a few seconds; twist the nipples as though trying to find a radio station for approximately one minute. Next move down to the hips and if she tries to give you any instructions as to what to do, ignore them. Just whisper in her ears, "Relax, don't worry. I know what I'm doing."

She shivered at the memory.

With Dominic she never knew what to expect,

which always heightened her sexual response. She missed making love to him. He'd once fulfilled her fantasy to make love in their walk-in closet—no lights and no talking.

Then there was the time when he gave her a blank book of coupons to write down her fantasies. This resulted in their making love three to four times a week for two months.

It couldn't hurt to be with him until her Mr. Right came along.

"So what do you think?" Dominic asked.

She turned to him, her decision clear. She walked up to him and kissed him, then slowly began unbuttoning his shirt. "I'll thank you some more, unless you have to be somewhere tonight."

He didn't move; his voice hoarse. "No."

"Good." She kissed him again.

He drew away and searched her eyes. "You're not going to regret this tomorrow, are you?"

"If you make me stop, you're going to regret it right now." She raised her mouth to kiss him again, but he kissed her first. His mouth enveloped hers while his hands unzipped her dress. It fell to a puddle at her feet. Brenda let out a moan of pleasure as his tongue caressed the inside of her mouth. She pushed his shirt off his shoulders.

"Tell me you want me," he said.

Her hand disappeared inside his jeans. "You tell me first."

He shut his eyes when she clasped him. "I want you."

She pulled down his jeans and arched into him. "I want you too."

Dominic removed the rest of his clothes and hers, then carried her to the sofa bed. He was right, they were like two elements irresistibly drawn together. When his bare flesh touched hers she thought she would shatter into pieces. She was alive. And so was he. She didn't realize how dead she'd started to feel inside, but not anymore.

She rolled on top of him and invited him inside her, knowing there was danger that he'd sneak back into her heart again. She didn't care. She didn't care about consequences or right and wrong. Right now she felt primal—she wasn't a creature of intellect, she was a creature of feeling and she'd experience as much as she could.

"Drive me home, baby," he whispered. "You know how."

She rocked against him driving him in and out until the frenzy between them rose to ecstasy. They changed positions, they kissed, they caressed, they made love until they fell away exhausted. Brenda stared up at the ceiling with tears streaming down her face.

Dominic touched her cheek. "What's this?"

"I'm happy to be alive."

"Me too, honey."

She tasted the saltiness of her tears. "Poor Madeline."

He tenderly brushed her tears aside. "Shh, don't think about her. Let's just be here now. Together."

"Yes." She drew him close, wanting to be as near him as she could. "Together."

Thomas dropped the phone as though it had just burned him and looked at Natalie as she read her book. "Do you know who that was?"

She turned a page without interest. "No."

He pointed to the phone as though it could come alive and bite him. "Dominic. He just gave me a holiday bonus."

"Why?"

"Because of the studio. He said everything went better than he'd hoped. How is that possible? The location sucks, the place is a dump. How could he be happy?"

"I don't know," Natalie said, then lifted her book to hide a smile.

"The book is real," Dominic said as he and Brenda lay on the bed in the studio. For the past three weeks they'd made use of the studio's sofa bed and nothing else.

Brenda's head rested on his chest. "I know."

He placed a hand behind his head. "We've been coming here for a while and you haven't drawn a thing."

"It's hard to work in the positions you force me in."

"I don't force you, you like them."

She raised her head. "True." She brushed her lips against his, then rolled away.

"We have to get to work," he said, his arm out-stretched and ready to pull her back in close.

"I know." She sat on the edge of the bed and looked down at him. "Think you can keep your hands off me?"

His fingers crawled up her back. "No."

She playfully removed his hand. "You have to."

He closed his eyes and groaned. "Get dressed and I'll try my best."

Brenda stood. "You know I've never tried drawing naked before."

"If you try that you won't be drawing at all."

She laughed and began to change. She pulled on a pair of jeans, a large T-shirt and tied her hair up with a tie-dyed head scarf.

"I can't work while you're here," she said as she adjusted her scarf.

"I promise to be quiet," Dominic said, his voice muffled as he pulled on a shirt.

"No. I need to be on my own."

He sighed. "You're probably right."

"I know I'm right."

He gave her a big wet kiss, then left. Brenda walked over to the drawing table and touched all the pencils, brushes and charcoal, then she sat. *I can do this.*

She picked up a specimen and placed it down, then for the first time in years, she began to draw.

In early winter Brenda surprised her team and business associates by hosting a catered event held in an intimate dining room, on the top floor of one of Seattle's finest hotels. She looked stunning as she stood near the entrance talking to the guests. She held her hair back with a satin headband and wore a full-length, sleeveless pink silk dress, with a scalloped neckline and a pair of matching low heeled pumps. A pair of emerald earrings completed the ensemble. She didn't realize the captivating image she made. She was too busy worrying about the man watching her from across the room and the last conversation they'd had.

"What do you mean I'm not invited?" Dominic said as Brenda checked her reflection in her closet mirror. He stood in the doorway and watched her.

She adjusted her hair. "You're not invited."

"Why not?"

"Because this event is about business. I want to announce how we've been funded, that's all."

He sat on the bed exasperated. "I'm paying for a party I can't even attend?"

"You're not paying for anything."

"You wouldn't be able to have this party if it wasn't for me."

She kissed him on the forehead. "And I'm very grateful." She looked at her reflection again. "But I think it is better that you remain an anonymous investor."

"And remain the anonymous man in your life."

She turned to him wary. "What do you mean?"

"Don't think I haven't noticed that we don't go out together. We don't go to restaurants, or movies or anywhere people may see us."

"We both have busy lives. I thought you were happy."

"I am happy," he said. "I'm just making a few observations."

"It's too soon. If you come with me, people will start asking questions and I'm not ready for them."

"There won't be any questions when people see us. The reason why we're together will be obvious." He stood and rested his hands on her bare shoulders and stared at her reflection in the mirror, his voice soft. "Do you honestly think I'd let you go out dressed like this without a chaperone?"

"I don't need a chaperone," she said in a tight voice.

His dark eyes met hers. "I'm coming."

"You're not coming."

He came.

Brenda smiled at her guests, determined to ignore him, although it was like trying to ignore a steak knife in a birthday cake. She could feel his gaze and knew anytime he moved about the room. He promised not to hint that they were a couple, but she worried that somehow their secret might be revealed.

"This is a wonderful event," Chuck said, his face shiny from too much champagne. His wife Sandy, a small petite woman, stood beside him, her strong grip keeping him steady.

"I'm glad you like it." She sent Chuck a look of censure. "Just don't like it too much and remember to eat something."

"We don't get out much," Sandy said with apology.

Chuck shook his head. "We don't get out at all." He leaned towards Brenda, his green eyes bright, but his tone sober. "I noticed Dr. Ayers is here. Is there a reason for that?"

Damn, she was afraid of that question. "He's interested in our research and I thought he could learn more by meeting the team."

Chuck seemed satisfied with her explanation and turned around to look at Dominic. "I could talk to him right now."

"I don't think now is a good time."

Sandy took her hint. "Yes dear, I'm hungry. Let's go to a table." She dragged Chuck away.

After speaking to a few more people, Brenda approached the podium. "I'm thrilled everyone could make it tonight. I wanted to have this event to honor you—those of you who are on this project and those of you who have supported us throughout the years. That is why it is my honor to announce that our project has been funded for the next two years."

A round of applause filled the room followed by congratulatory hugs and kisses.

"Also, Dr. Lawson has been promoted and will be hiring an assistant."

More applause sounded. Chuck ducked his head in embarrassment.

"Now I'm not going to keep you," Brenda said once the noise died down. "I just hope that you will enjoy yourselves and keep up the good work." She stepped down and Kendell approached her.

"My wife was sorry she couldn't make it."

"That's okay. I'm glad you could."

"I had something I wanted to tell you," he said with excitement.

"What?"

"Dr. Franklin has asked me to co-write a paper with him."

Brenda glanced down at her hands and searched for a reply. "Are you sure you want to do that with your busy schedule?" she asked in a cautious tone.

"Are you kidding me? This is my chance. Think of the opportunity. I get to have my name published with someone established. I can smell *tenure*."

"I just think you should think it through."

"I have. I'm going to give him my response next week." He frowned. "I thought you'd be happy for me."

"I am," Brenda said forcing a smile, not knowing how honest to be with him. "Really. It's just—"

"I know you're worried about my schedule. Don't worry, I'm doing better this quarter. Only three classes and a lab."

That was still quite a load considering the other activities he was involved with, but she didn't want to disappoint him. "Great. Good luck to you." She hugged him.

He hugged her back, then kissed her on the cheek. "Thanks and congratulations."

Brenda watched him walk away wondering if she'd led him to the slaughter.

"Who was that?" Dominic said beside her.

She jumped, then sent him a withering glance. "I told you to stay away from me."

"I have stayed away."

"I mean *all* evening."

He rested a hand on his chest. "You're hurting my feelings."

"I'll hurt a lot more if you don't move."

"I love your threats." He bent down and whispered in her ear. "They only excite me."

"What do you want?"

He glanced at Kendell. "Who is that man?"

"If you haven't noticed he's too young for me."

"I didn't notice. What I *did* notice is that he made you look worried."

"I am," she said, relieved to admit the truth.

"Why?"

"That's Dr. Baldwin. He wants to write a paper with Franklin."

"And you told him not to?"

"No."

"Why not? Why are you protecting Fink?"

She hit him in the arm. "Don't call him that in public."

"No one can hear us. Besides he should have been exposed years ago."

"It's not that easy."

"You're making it difficult."

"It will just look like I'm jealous and trying to pull down a well-respected scientist. He's done so much and so many years have passed."

"At least tell him," Dominic said looking in Kendell's direction.

She rubbed her hands together, uncertain. "I can't. He might not believe me."

"Want me to do it for you?"

"No, maybe Fink—I mean Franklin—has changed."

Dominic looked unconvinced. She didn't blame him, she didn't believe it either.

"I don't want to bring up the past if I don't have to. Franklin has helped a lot of careers and perhaps that's what he plans to do with Kendell. If this is his chance I don't want to ruin it for him."

Dominic shook his head as he watched the younger man laughing with other guests. "For his sake, I hope you're right."

Winter brought snow; spring brought rain but Brenda and Dominic had little else to worry them. They collected driftwood in Ocean Shores, shopped at Pike Place Market, and spent as much time as they could hiking in the mountains and sailing. The book progressed well and their affair even better, although as spring became summer friction in their perfect union started to show.

"I need a date," Dominic said, grabbing a drink from Brenda's refrigerator.

She looked at him from her position at the kitchen

table where she was reviewing two of Kendell's papers and a proposal for a book. "Then get one."

He sat down in front of her. "That's why I'm asking you."

"I can't go."

He leaned back and watched her with a hooded look. "Yes, you can," he said quietly. "You just don't want to."

"No, I don't."

"Why not?"

"I told you why before."

He shook his head with frustration. "Honey, we can't keep doing this. People are going to have to know soon. Why not now?" He reached out and covered her hand. "Come with me."

She pulled her hand away. "No. Please don't ask me again."

"I don't care what anyone thinks. Our lives are none of their business. If someone asks me about us I'll answer them, if I want to. And if I don't feel like it, I won't. It's not a big deal to get back with your ex."

"It's a big deal to me." *You don't know what it's like to be in your shadow.*

"Well, it's time to get used to it because I'm not going to start attending a whole bunch of events alone because you don't want to be seen with me. In several months I'll be guest of honor at the Monahan Awards. I want you there."

"Is that an ultimatum?"

"No, it's a choice. You either go out with me or I announce our relationship on TV." He stood and went to the living room.

Brenda stared at her fridge feeling trapped. She should end it now. She'd been with him for a lot longer than she'd planned. With him back in her life she hadn't given herself a chance to meet her ideal man. She had to be in control of this. She wouldn't allow him to make demands. No matter how good it felt she knew she would have to end the affair soon and quickly, before anyone found out.

Unfortunately, the next day, somebody did.

Chapter 11

"Clement!" Brenda gaped at her brother as he stood on her doorstep wondering if she should run into his arms or shut the door in his face.

He stared at her equally surprised. "What the hell happened to you?"

"What do you mean?"

He gestured to her leather pants and fitted purple top. "I came to check on you. You look different." He couldn't stop staring at her.

"I decided to make a few changes in my life."

"I can see that." He blinked as though trying to adjust his focus. "You look great!"

"And I've decided to take a few chances."

"I'm glad to hear it. You can't stay safe all your life."

"Right." She bit her lip, her pleasure at seeing him disappearing into a slight panic. "There's something you should know."

Clement lifted his suitcase. "Aren't you going to let me inside?"

"Well, that *something* I want to tell you about is inside."

Clement grinned. "You have a boyfriend. That's okay. I'll be very nice to him." He pushed past Brenda and set his suitcase down in the hallway. "What does he do? Is he a scientist?"

She closed the door. "No."

"You look nervous. Don't you want me to meet him?"

"Well…"

"You have nothing to worry about. Even if he's a dull taxidermist I'll pretend to be interested as long as he makes you happy."

"He does make me happy."

"Then that's all that matters." Clement walked toward the kitchen. "Where is he?" he asked, then stopped stunned when he spotted Dominic on the couch. "What are you doing here?"

"We're working on a project together," Brenda said quickly.

Dominic sent her a look, but didn't reply.

Clement nodded. "I see. I guess that's understand-able. It's just business." He walked into the kitchen and grabbed a bottle of water, then went back to the living room and sat on the arm of the couch. "So Dominic, what do you think?"

"About what?"

"Brenda's new man. She's trying to hide him from me, but she'll have to introduce us at some point."

Dominic watched Brenda, but she refused to meet his gaze. "She doesn't have to."

"Why not?"

"You've already met him."

Clement paused with the bottle to his lips, then slowly set it down. "What do you mean?" He turned to Brenda. "What does he mean?"

Brenda lowered her gaze.

"Tell him, Brenda, or I will," Dominic said.

Brenda raised her gaze and looked at Clement, pleading for him to understand. "I'm seeing him."

"Seeing who?"

"Dominic."

Clement slowly stood. "I see. Excuse us," he said to Dominic, then grabbed Brenda's arm, dragged her into the nearest bedroom and slammed the door. "Are you out of your mind?"

"I can explain."

"There's nothing to explain! That man shouldn't be here. You're supposed to have a new man in your life. Dammit, I knew I should have come and seen you sooner. I knew you wouldn't have handled your friend's death as well as I thought."

Brenda sank onto the bed. "I've recovered from Madeline's death and I'm happy."

"By seeing your ex? By spending time with the man who made you cry on more occasions than I can remember?"

"He's changed. It's different now."

Clement threw up his hands. "How?"

"He's more considerate. He listens. We don't argue as much as we used to."

"If you're so pleased with your relationship with him, why didn't you tell me about it?"

"My schedule's been busy."

"You're lying to me because you're ashamed and you should be ashamed."

"Why should I be ashamed?"

"Because you know it's wrong and you're doing it anyway. I mean look at you. This whole thing is obviously about sex. You know there's nothing else to keep you together."

"That's not fair."

"Did he ask you to dress like that?"

"What's wrong with this? I wanted to be sexy

today. Sometimes I want to be demure; sometimes I want to be plain. But I dress this way to please myself and you have no right to judge me."

"So are you going to marry him again?"

She headed for the door.

He blocked her. "Are you?"

"No."

"So it is just sex."

Brenda narrowed her gaze. "And what if it is? Does that make me a bad person? Is it wrong to want to have someone warm to go to sleep with and wake up to? Someone to travel with on weekends, someone to call when the workday is long?"

Clement stared at her appalled. "You're falling in love with him again."

She stepped back from him. "No, I'm not."

"But it's serious between you, I can tell."

"We're just having fun."

"You don't know how to have this kind of fun." Clement grabbed her shoulders. "He's wrong for you, Brenda."

She yanked free from him. "You hardly even know him. When we got married you were barely out of high school."

"I still remember him and he doesn't look like he's changed. I thought you were ready for something different in your life."

"I am."

"Then find someone else." He opened the door and left.

Brenda remained in the bedroom, trying hard to regain control of her emotions. She wasn't falling in love with Dominic again. Why did Clement have to come and ruin things? No, she wouldn't let him. She had a good thing going and she would end it when she wanted to, not because someone else told her to. She took a deep breath, then walked into the living room.

She saw Clement and Dominic sitting on opposite ends of the couch. The two men were opposites in many ways. Dominic was older, bigger and more dominating than Clement and made the younger man look almost boyish in comparison.

"So what's the verdict?" Dominic asked.

Brenda sat in an armchair. "Verdict?"

"Are you going to ask him to leave or are you going to ask me to leave?"

"I'm not going to ask anyone to leave."

"So that little private shouting match you had wasn't about me?"

"We weren't shouting," Brenda said.

Dominic raised his brows.

"We were just talking loudly," she added lamely.

Dominic turned to Clement. "You don't like me."

"He didn't say that," Brenda said.

Dominic ignored her. "And you don't trust me."

Brenda shook her head. "He didn't say that either."

Dominic glanced up as though searching for something. "There seems to be an annoying mosquito in the room." His stern gaze landed on her.

She bit her lip.

Dominic stood and said to Clement, "Let's go outside."

Brenda jumped to her feet. "Okay."

"Not you. Just us." He gestured to the patio. "You first."

Clement sent him a wary look but nodded and headed to the back. Brenda grabbed Dominic's arm before he could follow. "What are you going to do?"

"I'm just going to talk to him."

"Promise?"

He looked at her, stunned. "What do you *think* I'm going to do to him?"

"I don't know," she said, helpless. "You could lose your temper."

He folded his arms. "I'm starting to lose it right now."

"Just listen to what he has to say. He only worries because he cares about me."

For a moment he studied her, then said quietly, "And you think he's the only one?" He didn't give her a chance to answer. He walked to the patio and closed the glass door behind him.

At the sound of the door closing Clement turned and faced him as though prepared for a fight. Dominic sighed and pointed to a seat. "Sit down."

"Why?"

"Because I want to talk to you."

"I prefer to stand."

"Fine." Dominic took a seat and sat. "I'm glad you came."

"What do you mean?"

"We couldn't keep our relationship quiet much longer and now we don't have to."

"What's your game, Ayers?"

"I suggest you take a seat because I'm going to tell you a story."

"I prefer to stand."

Dominic sent him a hard look. "It's going to be a long story and you're going to listen to every word of it."

Clement reluctantly sat.

Dominic gazed out at the water. "I ran away from home when I was fifteen."

"I know that."

Dominic slanted him a fierce glance.

Clement settled back in his seat. "I'm listening."

"Life was never the same after my father left. Only three months after he'd gone my mother brought home Uncle Julius. He wasn't my real uncle but that's what I was supposed to call him. Then other 'uncles' followed, each worse than the last. But my mother wasn't particular—she liked a man in the house and as I got older, I got in the way so I left—just like my father had done." Dominic let out a deep sigh.

"I came to live with my aunt here in America in hopes of a better life," he said with a bitter grin. "I discovered that my mother's sister wasn't much different from my mother, but at least I had an ally this time, my cousin Thomas. We left his mother's house a couple years later. He worked while I went to school, then I worked while he went to school. We were determined to succeed and promised each other that we'd stay bachelors. We'd never get caught like the men trapped in our mothers' nets. He never did."

Clement stared at him confused. "What does this have to do with Brenda?"

"Nothing. It has to do with you."

"Me?"

"Yes. I can always spot a man who is running away from something."

Clement frowned. "Running away?"

Dominic nodded. "Your showy display of concern for your sister is touching, but that's not why you're here. What's going on?"

Clement stared out in the distance.

Dominic shrugged. "Of course you don't have to tell me."

"I quit my job."

"Okay," Dominic said, then waited.

"Brenda was always telling me that I should stand up to my boss and that I didn't need to be bullied by him. One day I couldn't take it anymore and left."

"And you have no other options?"

He shook his head.

"A man doesn't go to his sister in hopes that she'll take care of him."

Clement's jaw twitched with anger. "That's not why I'm here."

Dominic looked at him unmoved.

"Okay," he admitted. "Perhaps I had hoped she could help lead me in the right direction. She's always been good at that."

"What are you planning to do?"

"I didn't think of anything."

"I'm going to tell you what you're going to do. You're going to spend a couple of days with your sister, as though nothing has happened. Then you're going to return home and call me. I have a division in Oregon and can find you an excellent position in our engineering division, but you have to promise me to show up and work hard."

Clement stared at him in wonder. "Why would you help me?"

Dominic stood. "I think the reason's obvious, but

if you don't know you'll figure it out." He opened the patio doors.

Brenda rushed up to them and sent Clement a nervous look. "Is everything all right?"

"Everything is fine," Dominic said.

Brenda looked at Clement for reassurance and he smiled. "Yeah, just like he said."

Brenda clapped her hands together. "Good, because I've just had a great idea."

"What?"

"Tomorrow night I'm going to cook both of you dinner."

Chapter 12

"Is it okay to be afraid?" Clement asked the next evening as he and Dominic faced each other as they sat at the dinner table. The table was elaborately set and they could hear Brenda humming in the kitchen.

"I'm sure it will be okay," Dominic said, not sure at all.

Clement played with his fork. "Should I ask her what she's making?"

"Do you want to be disappointed?"

"No."

"Then don't ask."

"She's been at it for hours. Have you seen her?"

Dominic couldn't have helped seeing her. After coming back from work, he'd stepped in the kitchen and had seen Brenda wearing a crisp, black apron and gloves. All she needed was protective eye gear and she'd look like a blacksmith instead of a chef. "Yes, I saw her." He pointed at Clement. "But whatever she makes, we're going to pretend to enjoy it."

"No matter what?"

"As much as we can."

Brenda called out to them. "It's almost ready."

Both men groaned.

Minutes later, Brenda came out with a casserole dish, set it on the table, then left. Clement and Dominic leaned forward and looked at it.

"What the hell is that?" Clement whispered.

"Damned if I know."

Clement lifted his fork to poke it, but Dominic kicked him and he set the fork down.

Brenda returned with a bowl of vegetables. "You don't have to wait for me," she said in a bright voice. "Fill your plates." She set the bowl down, then left again.

"You first," Clement said.

"Coward."

Clement held up his hands in surrender. "I admit it."

Dominic took a deep breath, then picked up a

spoon and cut into the casserole mixture. "It looks like it has spinach, pasta and cheese. Maybe it's supposed to be lasagna."

"It doesn't look like lasagna," Clement said as he watched the mixture fall on Dominic's plate.

"It doesn't look like anything," Dominic said, putting the same mixture in front of Clement. "But we're still going to eat it."

Brenda joined them at the table, her gloves and apron gone. "Good, you've filled your plates. Now eat up."

Dominic picked up his fork. Clement watched in mounting horror until Dominic sent him a warning glance and Clement hastily lifted his own.

Dominic took a bite, hoping he could stomach the entire meal, then stopped. It tasted good. He took another bite just to make sure. "This is delicious."

"Yes," Clement said, just as surprised. "When did you learn to cook?"

"I've been practicing," Brenda said with pride.

"It's a miracle," Clement said, then winced when Dominic kicked him in the shin. "I mean amazing."

"Thank you. Are you sure you can't stay another day?"

Clement shook his head. "No, I've got to get a few things done."

"That's odd. You packed a lot of things for planning to stay a short while."

"Uh…yes, well…I just came to check on you and I see you're doing well."

Brenda smiled and looked down, missing Dominic's nod of approval.

That evening Brenda invited Clement to see her studio. She loved being there and wanted to share it with him. She loved the ambience, meeting the other artists in the building, the smell of paint and turpentine, and the scent of sawdust coming from the woodcarver's studio. She let Clement sit at her drawing table and showed him some of her illustrations.

"These are amazing," he said. "Why didn't you pursue this line of work? You are a fabulous biological illustrator. You could make a lot of money, and wouldn't have to spend your time sweating all day in a lab or searching for funding."

"I had wanted to pursue my art, but Mom didn't approve."

"Mom doesn't approve of a lot of things."

"I know, but I understand. She wanted a career in science before she became a stay-at-home mom. She didn't regret her decision, but encouraged me to pursue her passion. Besides, at that time, she didn't see a future for me as an artist. And you know how Dad is."

"Yes." Clement sighed. "He doesn't like men who are too soft and women who are too hard."

"Right, he always told me that I shouldn't get too educated because men don't like women who aren't feminine."

"Yet despite them you pursued both science and art."

"I know. Remember, by the time I graduated from high school, Dad had left private industry and accepted a position as a visiting professor at the university in the science department. Since I was the only one in the family interested in the same field as he was, he threw away his own advice regarding the role of a woman, and encouraged me. Throughout my undergraduate years, I got to do illustrations for several of his colleagues and got paid. Although he was proud of my talent, he was proudest of my accomplishment as a scientist. And so am I."

"That still doesn't answer why you stopped drawing."

She thought about her brief freelance career: the disappointments and struggle as she watched Dominic's career soar. It had forced her to face the fact that there were better artists than her out there. "I just found something better to do."

"I guess I was wrong."

"About what?"

"Dominic is good for you if he can bring you back to this." He gestured to the intricate drawing.

"What did he say to you on the patio?"

"He'd kill me if I told you and I'm starting to like him."

"Really?"

"Yes." He shoved his hands in his pockets. "I came up here to think about a few things and I've made a few decisions. I'm leaving my job."

She hugged him. "That's wonderful. I knew you could do it. What are you going to do next?"

"I'll tell you when things work out. I guess we're both making changes in our lives."

"Yes."

He lifted an image of Dominic Brenda had on her table. "And sometimes it's okay to go back to something familiar."

"One. Two. Three. Catch!" Sonya threw her wedding bouquet to the crowd of eager women fighting for their chance to grab it. Brenda stood to the side, looking regal in a turquoise blue drop-waist sheath dress, with a hand-painted silk shawl depicting an orchid, a pair of transparent three-inch high shoes and her third pair of stockings: ultra sheer shimming gold thigh-highs.

She watched the event in amusement. The wedding had been everything she'd expected and more. The bride and groom had written their own vows, which they sang to each other with the help of one of their friends playing a guitar. Brenda, and everyone there, was pleasantly surprised by the fact that they both could sing.

The color theme for Sonya's wedding was yellow and blue, and she'd asked everyone to wear these colors. It was an outdoor wedding, held on the grounds of a historical estate. The chairs and tables were decorated with flowers and ribbons, and all the ladies were given white carnations, while the men were given yellow ones.

Sonya looked radiant in an exquisite cream bridal gown with an extremely long veil. The groom wore a dark blue tuxedo trimmed with gold. Luckily, the service itself was short, with only the sniffles of Sonya's mother heard throughout.

The reception was held directly afterwards and featured a live steel pan band. Brenda was in no mood to dance, but enjoyed watching others. Chuck tried several moves, and bowed out early in the evening. Several men tried hitting on Brenda, most of them much younger than her, but she kept her distance, as best as she could, by always having something in her hand and looking like she was eating.

When Sonya saw Brenda, she introduced her to her entire family as though she were a celebrity. Eventually, Brenda was able to excuse herself and find Chuck and other members of her team to mingle with.

She remembered her wedding day. There hadn't been a big party—to her mother's disappointment—because they'd gone to the Justice of the Peace. It had been her happiest moment. She'd looked at Dominic and pledged her life to him and for a brief moment, as she saw the women fighting for the bouquet, she wished to have the chance to be a bride once again.

The shock of the realization surprised her. Marriage had never been in the forefront in her mind until that moment.

Could she marry again? Yes, her heart whispered. She glanced around the room, looking at the available men and felt nothing. Before, she would have been looking for her Ideal Man, but an inner voice whispered that she'd already found him. He'd been there all the time.

It had been two months since Clement's visit and since then she and Dominic had gone out together and she'd been able to handle being in his presence again. Yes, she could marry him.

But what if he never asked her? Would this affair be enough for her? And if he did ask her, would she say yes? Could things be different this time? Or would marriage change everything as it had before?

"Why didn't you try for it?" a man said next to her. She turned and gasped in horror. It was Wallace, the coffeehouse bore.

"What are you doing here?" she asked. She'd only meant to think it, but the words burst from her mouth.

Wallace smiled, assuming her surprise meant she was glad to see him. "I'm a friend of the groom."

Poor Robert. "I see."

"I've been meaning to talk to you again. I'm sorry about how things ended the last time we saw each other."

"I thought it was fine."

He looked hopeful. "You mean you didn't mind the way I spoke to him?"

Brenda furrowed her brows. *"Him?"*

"Yes, Ayers. I know I was a bit brusque with him. I hope he doesn't hold any hard feelings. I'd hate to upset him in anyway."

"Why?"

He cleared his throat. "Well...because I was hoping you could put in a good word for me."

"Why me?"

"Because you're seeing him. I'm working on this great idea that I know he'd be interested in funding and..."

She didn't hear the rest. She'd heard it before numerous times and it only reminded her of what being Dominic's wife's meant. It meant going to award banquets in his honor, being asked about his work instead of hers, it meant being invisible again.

* * *

"I thought I told you to schedule it for next week," Dominic told Thomas as they walked down the corridor of Ayers Corporation. "Today I was planning to take Brenda out."

"Nope, it's today. Sorry, we must have gotten our communication mixed up."

Dominic pushed the door to his reception office open with such force that Natalie jumped. "You know that's been happening a lot lately." He stopped and looked at Thomas. "I would hate to think it was on purpose."

"Why would I want to do that?"

Dominic stared at him for a long moment. "I'm beginning to wonder myself."

"It's going to be a short meeting. I'm sure Brenda will understand. Just tell her it's my fault." Thomas pointed at Natalie. "Call Brenda and tell her that Dominic will be running a little late. Then order some flowers and have them delivered." He turned to Dominic. "She'll be putty in your hands when you arrive."

"Don't send her flowers," Dominic corrected.

"Send her candy then," Thomas told Natalie.

Dominic shook his head. "No, she's not into them. I'll send her something else later."

Thomas glanced at his watch. "Come on. Let's get the folder so we can leave."

Dominic disappeared into his office, then emerged holding a manila folder. "Okay, let's go." They left the reception room and were halfway down the hall when Natalie came running after them.

"Dominic!"

He spun around. "What?"

"It's Brenda—she sounded funny on the phone."

"Funny how?"

"Distracted as though she wasn't really paying attention. That's not like her."

"No," Dominic said, understanding her worry. "It's not."

Thomas rolled his eyes. "She's probably just annoyed that you cancelled. Come on, Dominic."

"Please, Dominic," Natalie said. "I think you should talk to her. I still have her on the line."

Thomas tapped his watch. "We have to get to our meeting."

Natalie glared at him. "Brenda's more important."

"Brenda can handle things herself. Dominic, we've got to go. I'm sure it's nothing."

Dominic looked at Thomas, then Natalie and made a decision. He handed Thomas the folder. "Go without me. I'll meet you there," he said, then ran back to the office. He grabbed the phone. "Brenda?"

"Dominic?" she said, confused. "I was just talking to Natalie before she put me on hold."

"Yes, she came and got me. Is something wrong?"

Brenda hesitated, then said, "I didn't think so at first, but now I'm not sure."

"Why?"

"There's a funny smell."

"Like what?"

"Like gas, but it couldn't be gas. It's something else."

He gripped the phone. "Like what?" She gasped and his blood ran cold. "Brenda?"

"Oh no. Oh my God."

The line went dead.

Chapter 13

Controlled chaos greeted Dominic as he drove close to Brenda's house. Firefighters rushed in and out of the house, EMTs checked for victims, while the police fought to keep spectators at bay, but he didn't care about any of them. He just wanted to make sure Brenda was okay.

"Sir," a police officer said, blocking his path. "You have to stay back."

"I just need to know that she's okay."

"You'll find out soon."

"I want to find out now." He searched the area for a sight of her.

"Don't force us to arrest you."

"I don't care. I live here and I want to see my wife. Brenda!"

"I'm here!" a voice said. It was the sweetest sound he could have ever heard. She ran up the driveway toward him and he pushed passed the annoyed officer and gathered her in his arms. He closed his eyes, blocking out the house, the crowd and the noise, he just wanted to know that she was there safe with him in his arms.

"I'm okay," she whispered. An early autumn leaf fell from a nearby tree and danced across the lawn.

He knew he was holding her too tight, but somehow he couldn't let go. The last few moments had been hell, all the nightmares he'd imagined flashing through his mind, each one becoming more and more tragic.

"Please take me away from here."

He relaxed his hold.

"I will." He glanced up at the house; he saw the smoke and firefighters but didn't see any sign of burning. "What happened?"

"It was the water heater. It must have malfunctioned. They said it wasn't installed properly."

He staggered back as though he'd been shot. The water heater he'd had installed had nearly killed her?

"It probably had an error," she said quickly, seeing how her words hurt him. "This isn't your fault."

That wasn't good enough, he needed answers. He walked up to the Fire Marshall. "What's going on?"

"The water heater was most likely defective," he said. "It should never have been installed in the first place. But that's not all, there was no certificate evident."

"Certificate? What type of certificate?"

"Years ago, Seattle and surrounding suburbs implemented a law that all water heaters had to be installed by a bonded and licensed firm, and before being activated, had to be checked by someone from the county and have a certificate put on. There was none. It appears that this lady bought a bum heater and then had some friend of hers install it."

Dominic stood immobile, his mind racing and fueling his anger.

Brenda lightly touched his arm. "At least I'm all right."

He nodded, unable to speak.

Lincoln approached them shaking his head. "Thank God you're all right. You could have been killed."

"I know," she said, sending Dominic a worried glance.

"I heard of a story where the water heater burst and killed the entire family. Shot right through the roof and took the house off its foundation."

Dominic didn't move.

Brenda forced a light tone. "Yes, luckily my house is still standing."

Lincoln didn't take the hint. "What if it had happened while you were sleeping? Those fire fighters would be searching for your body."

"That's enough, Lincoln."

"Have you been checked out by the EMTs? You could have burns from the steam. Saw one guy with steam burns and his skin started peeling off."

"I'm fine," she cried when Dominic lunged for her. She stepped back and held up her hands. "Really, thanks." She led Dominic away before Lincoln could upset him more. "I'm telling the truth."

Brenda was briefly allowed into her house to gather some personal items. Luckily little damage had been done to the kitchen, and most of her clothing and furniture survived. Things she had stored in the basement were the ones that sustained the most damage, but the metal trunk survived intact.

Dominic helped her pack her car and his with what they could and then drove to his house. The events of the day had left her exhausted and he stayed with her until she fell asleep, but he knew he couldn't. He had something to tend to first.

* * *

Thomas leaped out of bed when someone pounded on his front door. Natalie woke up too.

"Who is that?" he asked her.

"I don't know, but you'd better answer."

Thomas waited. "Sounds like they're trying to bust the door down."

"Then answer it before they do."

"It could be a burglar."

"Burglars don't knock."

Thomas grabbed his robe and slippers, then marched down the stairs. He checked through the peephole and opened the door. He smiled. "Dominic, what brings you over at this hour?"

Natalie came up behind him, holding her robe tight. "Is something wrong?"

It was clear that something was wrong. Very wrong. Dominic looked furious. "I want to talk to you," he said softly.

Thomas placed a hand on his chest in surprise. "You want to talk to me? Couldn't you have just called?"

"Yes, but I didn't come over here to talk to you. I came over to beat the crap out of you, but I want to talk to you first."

Thomas swallowed, wondering if he was joking. "Would you like a drink?"

"No." Dominic walked past him, made his way to their family room and sat.

Thomas turned to Natalie. "Pour him something strong."

"But he doesn't—"

"Just do it."

She rushed away and he took a seat on the couch. "What is the problem?"

"Brenda is staying at my house because she can't stay at hers. Do you know why?"

Thomas shook his head.

"Because her water heater malfunctioned."

Natalie set the brandy down on the side table with a clatter. "My goodness, is she okay?"

"I found her watching firefighters securing her house, but yes, she's okay."

"Thank God for that," Thomas said.

"But I'm not okay. I don't like when my instructions aren't taken seriously."

Thomas forced a laugh. "It was an honest mistake. What do I know about water heaters? I had a friend of mine—"

"Stop lying to me. I know that you didn't give Brenda my messages. I later discovered that you didn't choose the loft, but that someone else did. You initially tried to place Brenda in a crime-infested back alley."

"That's not true."

"But someone else circumvented that. I learned it from the former owner who told me he spoke to a female. I thought there had been a misunderstanding so I investigated. When I learned he'd dealt with Natalie I assumed you'd given her the task instead. Now I know you didn't."

Thomas spun on Natalie. "What the hell did you think you were doing?"

She lowered her head.

"Why are you shouting at Natalie for saving your butt?"

"Look, the studio thing was just me trying to find a place fast and this heater business was an accident. I didn't know the damn thing would blow. I thought he was a professional and I was trying to save cost."

"Really?"

Dominic's unrelenting stare forced Thomas to be honest. "She was getting in the way. She's got you all confused again. Who's been there for you? Who was there when she left you? Remember that? Remember being handed your divorce papers? You think she's changed? She just wants your money. And I was going to make sure that she didn't get it."

Dominic leaped up and slammed Thomas against the wall. "You could have killed her."

"And you would have been better off."

"Maybe I should kill you instead."

"Go ahead," he scoffed. "At least I'd know she hadn't completely cut off your balls. You've gotten soft. We made each other a promise, remember? We weren't going to let any woman trap us, but you did. You were rising to the top faster than anyone I've known and then you let her back into your life and filled your time with dinners and dancing.

"Does she even know you're up for the Monahan Award? That next week you're going to be honored by your peers?

"Yes, but will she be by your side? Of course not. She doesn't want to hear about your accomplishments. She was always jealous of you. Now as much as before. Everything's fine between the two of you when it's all about her. She's with you when it suits her. I noticed she wasn't with you at the last two banquets. Do you like going alone?"

"That is none of your business."

"You are my business. You're my family. You know she's going to leave you again. You're holding on so tight because you know the moment you let go, she'll walk out of your life again. I sort of did you a favor with this water heater business. You get a chance to play hero. But what happens when she doesn't need you to rescue her anymore?"

Dominic stepped back and released him. "Yes, I see your logic."

"Good."

"You were just looking out for me as you always do."

"Right."

Dominic straightened his tie. "But you forgot about something."

"What?"

"You forgot to think about how I feel about her. You didn't think that her safety means more to me than my own life. Or yours." He turned to Natalie. "Will you please excuse us?"

Thomas stared at him. "What are you going to do?"

"You know you're fired."

"Yes."

He rolled up his sleeves. "Good, then I've finished talking."

Natalie jumped up from her seat on the stairs when she saw Dominic come out of the room. "Is he okay?"

Dominic sent her a cool glance, then said, "He'll live."

She nodded.

He headed for the door, then stopped and looked at her, curious. "Why do you stay?"

She shrugged. "Convenience, but I'm not going to stay anymore."

"Good, because I would like to hire you."

"Me? To do what?"

"Be my manager."

She shook her head, frantic. "But I couldn't do that."

"You've already done it," he said calmly. "It takes a clever woman to outsmart a man like Thomas. And I wouldn't have been there for Brenda if you hadn't made me talk to her. I didn't hire you to be my assistant because Thomas asked me, I hired you because I knew you could do the job. Now, you're getting a promotion. What do you say?"

Natalie hesitated, then asked, "Are you going to ask her to marry you again?"

Dominic paused. He hadn't expected that question. "It's still too soon."

"You're afraid she'll say no."

Dominic folded his arms and frowned with mock impatience. "You're supposed to manage my career, not my love life."

"One affects the other, and I want to make sure you're balanced. I could help you pick out rings if you want."

Dominic opened the door and couldn't hide a smile. "I'll let you know."

Chapter 14

Brenda called in to work the next day and told Chuck what had happened. After spending ten minutes calming him down she assured him that she was all right and that her house was still standing. Later that morning she and Dominic drove to the house. Thankfully, everything was not destroyed, but it was not livable. The steam and water had done its damage. She spoke to her insurance company and a restoration company came right away to assess all that needed to be done.

"Thousands of dollars worth of water damage," Brenda said with a sigh as she and Dominic sat in his sunroom. Sergeant sat by her feet. "I won't be able to go back for weeks."

"Don't worry. I'll cover it."

"My insurance will cover it and they'll pay for me to stay at a hotel."

Dominic stiffened. "Why would you want to stay in a hotel when you can stay with me?"

"I think it's better that I don't stay here."

"How can it be better? You should stay here. It's my fault your house got ruined."

"No, it's not your fault. You didn't know that it hadn't been installed correctly. I don't want what has happened to change things between us."

"Change what?" he demanded. Sergeant looked up at him worried.

"How things are working. This relationship has been great, but I think we should take it slow."

"Slow? We've been seeing each other for over six months. It's time we made a decision. I want you to move in with me."

Brenda shook her head. "I don't want to live with you."

"Then marry me instead."

She sat there blank. "What?" she choked.

"Marry me."

Brenda lowered her head. At last she'd heard the

question she'd wanted to hear, but her response surprised them both. "I can't."

"Why not?"

"Because you deserve better."

"What are you talking about?"

"I'm too ambitious. I want a name of my own and with you that's impossible. It's petty, it's wrong and I'm ashamed to say it but I don't want to be in your shadow again."

He stared at her, perplexed. "I don't understand."

"You're not supposed to because it's not your fault. You deserve a wife who will bask in the spotlight of being Mrs. Ayers. I never carried the title well."

"Thomas told me once that you were jealous of me and I didn't believe him."

"He was right. At that time I was jealous. Okay, I am still a little jealous, and it's an awful thing to admit." She looked at her hands because she couldn't look at him.

"Not really," he said, forcing her to look up in surprise. "I've been jealous of you. You were doing research and taking the time to really make a difference. While I did fluff, by making films and lots of money. I haven't been in a laboratory in years. I always admired your commitment to solving whatever problem you set out to."

"I haven't solved anything yet."

"But you will. My name may be famous now but one day your name will go down in history." He sighed. "I know I've been blind to a lot of things, and I know it's hard being connected to me. If I could change it I would, but I can't. But I promise you this, in our home only *we* will matter. You won't have to fight for my attention; you won't have to fight for my time. It will be yours." He gathered her hands in his and searched her eyes. "I want you back. Not as my lover or my girlfriend but as my wife. And I won't accept anything less." He let her go and stood. "I know it's a lot to think about so I'll give you time, but I won't have you staying in a hotel. I have a guest-house. You can stay there for as long as you need. In a week I'll ask you my question again. Your answer will determine whether I stay in your life or not." He left. Sergeant sent her a canine look of pity, then followed his owner.

Five days later Brenda sat alone in the guesthouse wondering how her life had come to this. A home that was presently uninhabitable, a man she loved but couldn't live with, and a life that suddenly seemed small. Nearly a year ago she had cared only about her project. Her entire existence depended on its success, but it no longer had that hold on her.

Months before, she'd been determined to find her

Ideal Man, now she had found him only to discover that *she* was the problem, not him. She didn't deserve all that he'd given her or the support of the club. She opened her wallet and looked at the membership card. She'd failed them. They'd done everything to help her and she had ruined everything.

She searched through her papers, found Rania's number and called her.

Rania picked up on the third ring. "Hello?"

"Hello, this is Brenda."

"Hi, Brenda, how are things?"

"I want to withdraw my membership from the Society."

Rania was quiet a moment, then said, "Why?"

"Because I don't have what it takes. I should be happy with my life, but I'm not. I have fantastic clothes, I learned how to cook, I'm back to illustrating and doing what I love, my project got the funds it needed, and the man I love asked me to marry him, but I can't marry him. I don't want to be a member anymore. This Society thing is wasted on me. Please write to whomever needs to be notified and remove all my privileges."

Rania laughed. "It doesn't work that way."

"What do you mean? Marci told me she could get my privileges revoked."

"Marci was exaggerating, but that's not the

problem. The problem is that you really don't know what marriage is all about. You're used to being center stage. You grew up as the only girl in a family of boys, you were always the smartest in the class. You haven't learned how to be with others without trying to compete. Marriage is about equals."

"That's the problem. We're not equals. Dominic was always better than me. I tried being a freelance illustrator and failed. He tried filmmaking and succeeded. I tried teaching and failed. He tried teaching and made an industry out of it. How can I compete with that?"

"Why do you need to?"

"Because I want to be noticed too. I need to be. I can't spend my life as just his helpmate. That's all my mother was. I'm not saying that there's anything wrong with being a wife and mother. They're important roles and she was happy. She *is* happy. But I don't want that for myself. I want more. I want to make a difference."

"You do make a difference every day. You've spent your life comparing yourself to Dominic so much you don't realize the lives you've touched. Not all of us are meant to be known around the world, see our names in papers and be heard on the radio. Dominic is like a tree. You're like a flower. Both have their place is this world and can live in harmony. Once you accept that your role is not as his shadow, but as his source, happiness will be yours."

"His source? His source of what?"

"Brenda, no matter how strong someone is, all anyone ever needs is to be loved."

Brenda thought about Rania's words as she worked late in her office. Tonight he expected an answer. She loved Dominic, but could she love him the way he needed her to? She had to go home and find out. She was about to shut off her computer when Franklin ran into her room.

"You have to help me," he said, terror filling his voice. "You have to make him understand. He trusts you and listens to you. Tell him I didn't mean to do it, it just happened that way."

"What are you talking about? Tell whom what?"

He searched frantically around the room. "Please, Brenda, help me hide."

"But I don't understand."

Seconds later Kendell burst into her office holding a knife.

Chapter 15

He looked awful, as though he hadn't slept in days. His expensive shoes were cuffed and the hole on his jacket sleeve had grown larger.

Brenda stared at him. "What is going on?"

"Get out of the way, Brenda," Kendell said. "This has nothing to do with you."

"Kendell, put down the knife."

He pointed it at Franklin. "I will after it has his blood on it."

"You don't understand," Franklin said, desperate. "I had to do it."

"You had to steal my ideas? You had to publish

three of my papers as your own? You had to take my book proposal and submit it under your name? You *really* had to do all that?"

"Look, they wanted an expert on the subject. I thought I was doing you a favor. I was going to hire you as a ghost writer and split the profits."

Kendell slowly approached him with the knife held out.

Franklin hid behind Brenda. "Do something! Talk to him."

"There's nothing she can say. You stole my work. I've slaved for months. You know my wife is divorcing me? She said that I spend too much time working. She doesn't get how important it is to me, but you do."

Brenda slapped Franklin's hand away when he clutched her arm. "Kendell, he's not worth it."

"I may lose my job," he said miserably. "My performance reviews aren't the greatest and I haven't published enough."

"I can make sure that doesn't happen," she assured him.

"I've given everything to this school and this is how I'm repaid."

"Your life is not over. You have a lot to live for. You can save your marriage and your career, but you can't do that from prison." She held out her hand. "Give me the knife."

"You're right," he said with an eerie resignation. "I wouldn't want to go to prison. It just doesn't seem that life is worth living." He turned the knife to himself.

"Oh no, you don't," Brenda said, knowing she couldn't face another suicide. She picked up a book and threw it at him as she would throw a football to one of her brothers. The book hit him on the side of the head, knocking him down. She grabbed his knife, then checked his injury as he lay on the ground dazed.

"Good aim," Franklin said.

"Shut up." She touched Kendell's forehead, then helped him sit up. "You'll be all right."

"He stole everything from me," he said in a broken whisper.

"We'll make sure he doesn't get away with it. I'll help you."

"You mean you believe me? He said no one would."

"He says a lot of things that aren't true." She helped him stand. "Go home and promise me you won't do anything stupid."

"I promise."

Brenda watched him leave, then turned to Franklin, who was adjusting his tie as though he'd just suffered an inconvenience instead of an attack on his life. "I should press charges," he said.

Brenda picked up the knife and looked at it. "I can understand why he would want to kill you."

Franklin looked at her as though she bored him. "Is that some sort of threat?"

"No, I could never stab you." She touched the tip of the knife. "But I remember how angry I was when I discovered you stole my work."

His eyes widened. "You knew?"

"Of course I knew."

"But you never said anything."

"No, but I'm going to say something now. I want you to admit your plagiarism and resign."

He laughed. "I'll do no such thing."

"Yes, you will." Brenda picked up the phone. He rushed over and stopped her.

"Who are you calling?"

"Why do you care?"

"Do you want money? I can give it to you."

"I want you to resign. Now."

"Where would I go? I'm established here. You can't do this to me." He straightened. "I bet you're just bluffing. You'll probably call Dominic, but he can't do anything to me. If he lays a hand on me, I'll sue. Besides he's gotten his revenge."

"What are you talking about?"

"I don't know how the bastard did it, but no other university will hire me. Why the hell do you think I've been stuck here all these years?"

"How do you know it was him?"

"We had a chat one day about you. I won't bore you with the details, but he explained a few things to me. I thought he was upset because I broke your heart." Franklin clenched his hands. "I'm meant for great things and he stopped me, but I've managed to get around his childish sabotage. And you see how I've succeeded."

"Yes, I see," she said quietly. She lifted the phone. "I'm not calling Dominic. I have my own connections."

He yanked it from her. "What the hell is this really about? So I put my name on two of your papers, so what? I made them better. I got them seen and I would have taken you places if you'd stayed with me."

She sent him a cold stare. "Resign."

He stared back with contempt. "Never, and there's nothing you can do about it."

Brenda sat behind her desk and clasped her hands together as though ready to give a lecture. "I reviewed all of Kendell's papers and have the rough drafts with my comments." She pulled out a thick file and waved it at him. "Think of how it will look if I make them available so they can be compared to your published articles?" She held his stare. "I also have my old papers. What do you say to that?"

Franklin took one step forward, fury in his eyes, then stopped as the reality of his defeat faced him. His shoulders fell and he walked away.

Brenda rested her head in her hands trying to

process all that had happened. She'd thought seeing Franklin lose everything would make her feel more triumphant, but a part of her felt sorry for him. His career and reputation was everything and now it was gone.

Brenda stood. Fortunately that wasn't how her life would be. She packed her things and left the office. When she went outside, she saw Kendell standing by her car. "I thought I told you to go home," she said.

"I wanted to thank you. I was blinded by rage and obsessed about all that he'd stolen. I'd really lost it."

"Things will work out." She gave him a hug.

Suddenly, he stiffened and she felt something was wrong, even before she jerked back and turned. Kendell's wife stood there, her soft dark curls surrounding a face filled with horror.

"I knew it wasn't just work," she cried. "Our marriage is over." She spun away.

Kendell started to run after her, but Brenda grabbed his arm and shouted at the woman, "Come back here. Now," in her most authoritative voice. The young woman stopped and slowly turned.

"Come on," Brenda said impatiently.

The woman walked toward them, then stopped a few feet away.

"I am flattered," Brenda said. "But there's nothing, absolutely nothing going on between us. The fact that you would think so is sad."

"Sad?" she said with a sour twist of her lips. She pointed to Kendell. "He's always here and he's always telling me how great you are. And all the things you're helping him with." Tears gathered in her eyes. "He talks as though this is his life."

"This is my life," Kendell said. "I want to be a great professor. I want to see my name in trade journals. You knew that when we got married."

"But what about me? I can't compete with this." She gestured to the expansive building and grounds.

"But I'm doing this for you."

"I don't want you to."

Brenda moved forward and took his wife's hand, sensing her pain. "I know how you feel. Years ago I divorced my husband for the same reason. I couldn't compete with his dream, but I never told him what I needed from him. I never gave him the chance to change. You're both making mistakes at this moment, but that can be fixed. Tell him exactly what you want. Don't make him guess."

His wife looked at him. "I want you to be home so we can eat dinner together. Do things on the weekend. I just want to be with you and talk about other things and not just about your work. Can you understand that?"

Brenda turned to him. "And what do you want from her?"

"I want her to listen—"

Brenda shook her head and forced him to face his wife. "Talk to her."

He took a deep breath. "I want you to listen to me when I talk about my career and not to pretend. I want you to understand *how* important this is to me."

Brenda nodded, pleased, and folded her arms. "Okay, now that you know what you both want, how can you fix it?"

Kendell sighed. "I won't schedule late classes anymore and I'll leave one day a month just for us. We can go on a date."

His wife nodded. "And I won't bother you about the time it takes you to grade papers or your late nights, but I want to select where we'll go on our dates." She tenderly touched his cheek. He wiped her tears.

Brenda rested her hands on her hips. "You love each other but you can't expect everything to be perfect. You have to work at it and the moment it becomes a competition, where one of you has to win, instead of a compromise where you work together, your marriage will end." She shook her head in regret. "I know."

"Thank you," Kendell said, putting his arm around his wife's shoulders.

She smiled at Brenda. "I can see why Kendell talks about you. You are wonderful. Thank you for everything."

"You're welcome."

Brenda watched them go, wishing someone had been around when her own marriage had hit a rough patch. But she was older and wiser now and had a second chance. She finally realized the one thing she'd never told Dominic throughout their marriage. She'd said *I love you, I want you, I need you,* but never the three words she now knew he needed to hear. She would have to tell him now. She would let him know he was the only man for her and that she didn't have to look any further.

With her heart bursting to tell him how she felt, Brenda pulled out her cell phone and dialed Dominic's number. Unfortunately, she couldn't reach him on his cell phone or at his office. She returned to the guesthouse, put her things down, then ran to the main house. Natalie came out the door just as she was about to knock.

"Brenda," Natalie said, surprised.

"Yes," she stammered, just as surprised to see her. "I wanted to talk to Dominic."

"He's not here. He's at the premier showing of his film on global pollution. You know, The Monahan Awards. But when he got there, I saw the horrendous tie he was wearing and begged him to give me his keys so I could get him another one."

He had mentioned his award. He was guest of

honor. She had forgotten about it because all his awards hadn't meant anything to her. She bit her lip, feeling awful. "Can I take it to him?"

Natalie smiled. "I'll help you dress."

Brenda thought about the gown in her metal box. "I know exactly what to wear."

Tonight he would get his answer, Dominic thought. He stood behind the black curtain with his yo-yo, unconcerned with what would happen in front of it. All he cared about was getting Brenda's answer. After his speech, he'd shake some hands and smile at a few faces, then go to the guesthouse and find out what his future held.

He glanced at his watch; he'd have to go on soon. Where was Natalie? She only needed to grab a tie. He had hundreds. Suddenly, in the darkness backstage he saw a silvery skirt come into view. He didn't remember Natalie wearing a skirt, but he hadn't been paying much attention. "Thanks, Natalie," he said, winding up his yo-yo.

"Want me to tie it for you?"

He stopped. That wasn't Natalie's voice. Dominic glanced up and stared at Brenda, astonished. She looked ravishing in a floor-length silver ball gown, with her hair piled high, wearing a pair of semi-precious stone hoop earrings and a pair of silver high heels.

"What are you doing here?" he said in a hoarse voice.

She draped the tie around his neck. "Fixing your tie."

He shook his head. "That's not what I mean."

"I'm here because I should be."

He frowned, not understanding her.

She kissed him. "Do you want your answer now or later?"

His heart began to race. "Brenda. I—"

The announcer's booming voice cut through his. "It is our privilege to honor the renowned Dr. Dominic Ayers this evening…"

Neither of them heard the rest of the introduction as they stared at each other. Dominic looked at her wanting to hear the word he'd been waiting a week for.

Brenda quickly hugged him then said, "Go out there and accept your award. I'm proud of you and it will be an honor to be your wife." She smiled. "Again."

He kissed her as though his heart would break if he let her go. She kissed him back with just as much passion, then pulled away. "You have to go."

"I love you," he said in a rush. "It's always been you. You stole my heart years ago and never gave it back. I'll make you happy and I'll make you proud. And I'll—"

She placed a finger against his lips. "You don't have to do anything. I love you just as you are." She pushed him toward the curtain. "Now go."

He sent her one last look before disappearing in front of the curtain to the thunderous sound of applause.

Chapter 16

Dominic was besieged by well-wishers and wannabes once the presentation was over. Brenda didn't mind. She stood silently beside him basking in the glow of his success. She smiled graciously, feeling genuinely happy for him and, for the first time, realizing his success was also hers. She no longer felt the need to compete or to be envious.

Four weeks later they were married. Nearly a year after that, their book, *An Introduction to the Fantastic World of Science,* hit the shelves and became a bestseller.

Brenda sat in her office staring at the picture of her

husband. She picked up the postcard she'd just received showing an aerial view of Alaska, lying on her desk.

Someone knocked. "Come in."

Dominic entered. "I'm taking you to lunch."

"I'll be with you in a minute," Brenda said, flipping the postcard over.

He walked behind her chair and rested his hands on her shoulders. "I thought I was the only one who sent you postcards."

"Are you jealous?"

"Depends who it's from."

"It's from Sonya. She's telling me about her new research project in Alaska."

"I know it was hard for her to leave you."

"Yes." It had surprised Brenda how much she missed Sonya's bouncy enthusiasm, clever mind and big heart. She quickly read the message then stopped when she saw a doodle sketched in the margins.

Dominic leaned closer and saw it too. "What's that? Looks like the state of Florida."

"No, it's not," Brenda said, then laughed. "It's a stocking. She knew!"

He frowned. "Knew what?"

Brenda slowly stood and rested a hand on her belly, feeling the new life that was growing inside her. She looked at Dominic, the man she'd nearly lost forever. "What I needed."

Kappa Psi Kappa—these brothers are for real!

Award-winning author
ADRIANNE BYRD
Sinful Chocolate

Dark and delicious…

When a doctor gives playa extraordinaire Charlie six
months, he tries to make things right with all the
women he's wronged. Gisella Jacobs is busy launching
her new shop, Sinful Chocolate, when delectable
Charlie knocks at her door. But when she starts falling
for him, she finds it hard to heed her girlfriends'
warnings—and harder to resist him.

*Coming the first week of January 2009
wherever books are sold.*

KIMANI™
ROMANCE

www.kimanipress.com
www.myspace.com/kimanipress

KPAB0970109

Summer just got a little hotter!

National Bestselling Author

MELANIE SCHUSTER

A Case for *Romance*

With all her responsibilities, Ayanna Walker
hasn't had time for romance…until now. While
Johnny Phillips wants to share the future with
Ayanna, she's thinking only one thing: hot summer
fling! Can a man planning forever and a woman
planning the moment find the right time for love?

*Coming the first week of January 2009
wherever books are sold.*

KIMANI™
ROMANCE

REQUEST YOUR FREE BOOKS!

2 FREE NOVELS
PLUS 2 FREE GIFTS!

KIMANI ROMANCE™

Love's ultimate destination!

KROM08R